Baildon Moor

A Novel

by

Rosanna Luke

with lots of
love and best wishes
Roz x

First published in 2017

This is a work of fiction. Names, characters, businesses, places, events and incidents are either the products of the author's imagination or used in a fictitious manner. Any resemblance to actual persons, living or dead, or actual events is purely coincidental.

British Library Cataloguing in Publication Data.
A catalogue record for this book is available from the British Library.

ISBN-13: 978-1542562713
ISBN-10: 1542562716

"It seems strange to write about these things now, but the time has probably come when we should accept whatever is past and gone and never will return."

New Model Army, "Modern Times"

Prologue

Bradford, West Yorkshire

15 October 2013

I wake up from the familiar nightmare and for a moment I don't know where I am, even though I'm lying in my bed at home. I touch my neck expecting to still feel the rough rope of the hangman's noose but there's nothing there. My heart is thumping, I'm hag-ridden and drenched in sweat and the sheets cling to me like a shroud. I fumble for the bedside light, sit up and take deep breaths until my pulse stops galloping.

The alarm clock says that it's a few minutes after five o'clock. From experience I know I won't get back to sleep so I peel off my nightshirt and pad into the shower, where I scrub the lingering dream away.

Wide awake now, I wrap myself in a fluffy dressing gown and go downstairs to the kitchen to make coffee. As I fill the machine Marwood appears from nowhere like a sloe-black ghost; he meows and slinks around my ankles. He butts his great blunt head against my legs and begins to purr.

I take my cup of coffee and sit on the sofa where Marwood kneads at my dressing gown, his green eyes half-shut with contentment as he digs his claws into the thick loops of cotton fabric. I put the mug on the glass table and rub his tattered, bald ears until he settles down back to sleep on my lap, his tail wrapped tightly around his nose.

I look at Marwood sleeping and feel something like jealousy. It's still only half past five and still far too early to go to work, so I pick up yesterday's paper from the table and flick through it.

Bradford Telegraph & Argus

14 October 2013

Human Skull Discovered on Baildon Moor

A human skull has been found by a local man walking his dog at an isolated beauty spot on Baildon Moor.

'We were walking by the old mine, like we do every morning,' said Les Carter, (56) from Bingley. 'Prince had run off and when he came back I thought it was an animal bone that he'd got, maybe from a sheep, but then I saw there were fillings in the teeth so I took it straight to the police station. It was horrible.'

A spokeswoman for West Yorkshire Police told the *Telegraph & Argus* "We can confirm that a number of suspected human remains were discovered around the Windy Hill and Bingley Road areas of Baildon Moor. Investigations continue and a full search of

> the area is being carried out. We urge any members of the public who may have information to come forward and call us on 101."

The article hits me like a punch: I start to shake and coffee spills from my mug. I put it back down on the table with a thud. Marwood wakes with an accusing chirrup when I scoop him up from my lap and move him to the sofa, where he circles twice and curls up like a bun.

Panicking now, I run to the bedroom and pull out the metal trunk from under my bed; it leaves rusty stains on the magnolia carpet and a cloud of gritty dust billows up as I drag it towards me. In the hurry to open it I cut my finger on the corner of the lid although I barely feel the pain through the rising wave of terror. Somewhere in here is my address book with Sullivan's phone number, years out of date but for both our sakes I have to let him know what has happened and warn him that the police will come and ask us questions about what happened that night.

I leaf through the trunk. There are layers of old pictures and letters, and some flyers that I'd designed for Sydenham Poyntz gigs. I pick up a faded photo of Sullivan, Rob, Jason and Simon, all happy and drunk, posed like a line-up against a grafitti'd breezeblock wall in an anonymous Bradford nightclub. Another photo, this one of Sullivan standing in front of an artificial Christmas tree, cigarette in hand and grinning at the camera. Billy, maybe sixteen or seventeen, is dressed all in black and brooding on the sofa. I recognise the front room of our old flat at West Bowling and the rush of nostalgia makes my head whirl.

Then there's a picture of me in fancy dress at a party somewhere: unbearably young, wearing a peach ball gown and a gold crown, my waist-length hair is crimped and dyed fuchsia pink; my eyes are lined with thick black kohl.

I put the photos to one side and dig down to the bottom of the trunk until I find what I'm looking for: an address book, bound in red and silver fabric and scuffed at the corners: addresses twenty years old for friends I've not seen or thought of for half a lifetime.

I flick through it, looking for an entry for Sullivan, but realise there's no point – he'll have moved and I don't even know whether he still lives in Bradford. I'll have to find another way to contact him, to tell him that someone has found Rudy.

I wonder whether he has nightmares, too.

PART ONE

Chapter One

January 1988

Nicole and I trudged across the campus back to her room. It was snowing: huge sleety flakes fell from a sky the colour of iron and the air was so cold it even tasted of metal. I shoved my gloved hands further into my pockets and felt grimly convinced I would never get the hang of Yorkshire winters.

Her housemates were in the kitchen listening to The Smiths on someone's portable cassette player. I already knew chirpy Geordie Diane and her boyfriend Simon-from-Essex, but there was another man I didn't recognise. He was stunning, an absolute vision: tall and willowy with dark eyes and long brown hair that spread in thick waves down his back. He wore tight black jeans, a purple paisley shirt and a leather biker jacket, all topped off with hooped earrings and dozens of thin silver bracelets.

'Oh...hi,' I stammered, suddenly aware of my wind-whipped hair and cold, red face. He looked at me for a second before replying and I felt my face flush even darker under his gaze.

'Hi,' he replied. 'I'm Sullivan.'

'Julia.'

I held out my hand for him to shake, I was suddenly shy and best-behaviour formal.

'How do you know Nicole?'

'I'm in a band with Simon,' he said. 'We're called Sydenham Poyntz. You should check us out some time.'

'Yeah, I'll do that. Definitely.'

Nicole brought me a mug of Nescafé, interrupting the moment. 'So, Julia, what do you reckon?'

'Sorry – I…I was miles away…you what?'

She laughed. 'I know.'

We drank our coffee in the warm hubbub of her kitchen. As Morrissey begged the shoplifters of the world to unite I kept sneaking sly glances at Sullivan. I was smitten.

A fortnight later I was buying a sandwich from the library snack bar when a photocopied black and white poster advertising a Sydenham Poyntz gig caught my eye. My heart did an involuntary somersault when I saw their name: I desperately wanted an excuse to see Sullivan again and here was a textbook opportunity. I made a mental note of the date and started to put a plan into action.

'There's a gig in the Communal Building on Thursday night,' I said to Nicole that afternoon after a particularly tedious History of Art tutorial. 'That band – what are they called? You know, the one that Diane's boyfriend is in. Do you want to come along?'

'Cool.'

I spent the next few days discreetly panicking, and on the Thursday night I took over three hours getting ready. I crimped and back-combed my hair to within an inch of its life, spent an age getting my smoky eye make-up just right and changed my clothes four times, finally settling on a black velvet mini-dress and my best Doc Martens.

Sydenham Poyntz's set was amazing: mostly cover versions of Sixties and Seventies classics – Led Zeppelin, The Who and Free. Nicole and I got right down the front by the amps and danced our socks off, but I nearly died from embarrassment when Sullivan caught my eye and grinned at me halfway through the guitar solo in *All Right Now.*

After the gig we were finishing up our pints of tepid cider when Sullivan appeared at my side. He smelt of warm leather and patchouli; I felt my knees give way a little.

'Evening, thanks for coming along tonight. Can I buy you both a drink?'

'Um, yeah, th...thanks.'

'Sorry, I'd love to stay, but I've got an essay due in the morning,' said Nicole. She flashed me a wink and headed off into the night.

Sullivan came back from the bar with two more pints in plastic glasses. We sat in a booth away from the smoke and noise of The Commie's illuminated dancefloor and we talked for the next three hours about pre-Raphaelite art and our mutual love of Dickens until we were the last people there at closing time.

It turned out that Sullivan was actually called Jeremy – a name he absolutely and passionately hated – and he came from Salford, where he lived with his mum and younger brother. He was studying English when he wasn't gigging with the band.

It was pouring with rain when we left the club, although I barely noticed. Sullivan took my hand and walked me home, and when he kissed me outside the student union I thought I would explode.

We swiftly became inseparable. We discovered a shared passion for long country walks and that spring we went hiking on the moors around Ilkley and Baildon. We walked for hours and ate home-made ham sandwiches sitting under the endless moorland skies, marvelling at how tiny and insignificant we felt against the landscape, and we came home footsore with our jeans and boots caked in mud. I snapped a photo of Sullivan on one of our hikes but when I got the film developed he was barely more than a speck silhouetted against a great grey crag.

Sydenham Poyntz had regular bookings every month at the student union bar. I went to every gig they played and got to know the other guys in the band: Sullivan and I spent so much time together that they nicknamed us the Siamese Twins.

'Are you going home for Easter?' I said to Sullivan on a March afternoon as we sat in Peel Park, sharing a bottle of Strongbow. The sun was starting to dip below the treetops and the lengthening shadows made the grass beneath my legs feel damp and chilly.

'I don't think so. I might go back for a weekend but there's no point otherwise, the rent's paid on my place for the whole year, it seems a shame to waste it. Anyway, I'd rather spend it here than at home with mum and Billy. Salford's boring.'

'Really? Oh, that's great.'

'What about you?'

'Same here, my room in halls is paid for in the holidays as well so I'm staying put.'

'You're not going home at all?'

'Bradford is home.'

'How do you mean? I thought you were from down South.'

I picked at the hem of my skirt and looked away. 'I'm not going back to Portsmouth. Mum and dad threw me out. It's a long story and when I moved here that was it, I made myself a promise that I'd never go back. So I haven't.'

He sat up and looked at me. 'You're joking? Why did they do that?'

'It's complicated, alright?'

'Go on, you can tell me.'

I took a deep breath and told him how mum started to hate me when I dyed my hair pink and started to wear black every day; about the time she found out I'd had the tattoo done on my shoulder; how she cried and shouted at me about what the neighbours would say if they found out.

Once I started I couldn't stop and the words poured out of me, tumbling over each other like water rushing over rocks. I told him about how my parents were both religious nuts – all God this and Jesus that – and explained about the scene that mum made when she found the deck of tarot cards in my sock drawer, and how it ended up with her marching me round to the vicarage for a lecture.

I squeezed my eyes shut and told him how my parents threw me out of the house one morning not long after I'd done my A-Levels, when I'd missed the last train home from London after a Cure gig and stayed out all night. I told him about dad telling me I was no better than a whore, with me standing outside the house in the rain with last night's make-up running down my face. How lucky it was that I passed my exams and made it to Bradford, vowing never to speak to them ever again.

I uncapped the bottle of cider, took several deep swallows and blinked away tears. I suddenly felt cold and shivered inside my leather jacket.

Sullivan kissed me on the forehead and told me he loved me.

By the middle of the summer term, I'd all but moved out of my room on campus and into Sullivan's gently reeking bedsit above a kebab shop.

'I've got to find somewhere to live,' I said to Sullivan one afternoon as we lay, tangled like otters in his single bed, sharing a joint and watching telly. 'Term's nearly over, we've all got to move out of halls by the end of the month.'

'Yeah, I suppose you do.'

'Why don't we get a place together? You know what they say about two being able to live as cheaply as one.'

He turned and looked at me. 'Really?' he said. 'Then let's do it. I hate this place; it stinks and it's like a rabbit hutch.' He made it sound almost romantic.

I took a deep drag on the joint and watched the smoke curl up towards the ceiling.

'It's Thursday today, isn't it?'

'Think so, why?'

'Thursday's when the *Telegraph & Argus* has the property ads.'

I handed the joint back to Sullivan; he took a final puff and stubbed it out in the ashtray next to his bed.

'Come on then, what are you waiting for?'

We threw on our clothes and went to the corner shop, bought a paper and raced each other up the three flights of fetid stairs back to his room. We collapsed, wheezing and giggling, back onto his bed.

'How about this one? "Double bedsit to rent, Stanningley".'

'No, I've had enough of bedsits.'

'Fair enough. What about "Two-bedroom house with garden, Saltaire"?'

He looked over my shoulder at the advert and whistled. 'Have you seen the price?'

'Ow. Too right.'

He took the paper from me and ran his index finger down the fine print.

'Here we are. One bedroom flat, West Bowling. Twenty pounds a week plus bills.'

I called the number that evening. The flat was still available so we met the landlord – a shrewish man who ran a chain of bookmakers – for a viewing the following day.

The flat had sludgy green carpets and there were shadows on the nicotine-yellow walls where a previous tenant had put pictures up. It came with a few bits and pieces of furniture that had seen better days: a grey settee with stained arms, a small double divan and a cheap pine coffee table. I loved it.

'What do you reckon?' I asked Sullivan as we looked around.

'Yeah, it's alright. At least it doesn't smell of kebabs.'

'Isn't it brilliant? I'm going to buy a throw to put over the sofa though. It's a bit manky.'

'Those walls need painting too,' he said.

'Yeah, but he might not let us. What if we put up our posters instead – your Stairway to Heaven and fractals ones can go in the living room, my Kate Bush and Robert Smith can go up in here...'

He groaned. 'Oh God, not Kate Bush, please.'

The flat felt like home to me already. We paid the deposit and moved in a fortnight later, our belongings stuffed into an assortment of laundry bags and transported across town in the back of Simon's red Escort.

That summer I met Billy for the first time when Sullivan's mum came to visit our new flat. Whilst Sullivan and I politely drank tea, Barbara filled him in on the news from home: which of his old school friends was getting married, who was expecting, who'd moved in two doors up into Mr Wilson's old house.

I tuned out and watched Billy, sitting cross-legged on the living room floor and engrossed in his football stickers. He was a scruffy-looking child with freckles and ginger hair.

He looked up at me. 'Are you my brother's girlfriend?'

I laughed. 'Yes, I'm Sullivan's girlfriend.'

'Oh,' he said and turned back to his Euro '88 stickers. He unpeeled a footballer and carefully placed him in his appointed place in the album.

'So, who's that?' I asked, and pointed to one of the players. I was genuinely trying to take an interest, but really didn't have a clue about football.

'*That's* Glenn Hoddle. God, you're so thick.' Billy rolled his eyes.

'Oi!' With a clatter of bangles Sullivan gently cuffed his younger brother across the back of his head.

'Billy! Don't speak to Julia like that.'

'Sorry.' Billy flushed bright red.

'So what do you want to do when you grow up?' I asked him.

'Dunno. But I want to go to university and be in a band like my brother.'

'But you're only thirteen!'

'There's nothing wrong with ambition,' said Sullivan. 'Mum and I use it as an incentive to get him to do his homework.'

Over the next two years, Sydenham Poyntz made a name for themselves in Bradford with their uniquely modern take on 12-bar blues. By the time we graduated the band had long since moved on from the Led Zep covers; by now they were writing their own songs and getting gigs most weekends. They played in pubs and clubs in Bradford and as far afield as Leeds and Halifax. Sometimes they even got paid.

I passed my degree in History of Art with a 2:1 and Sullivan got a third in English Lit. Between the two of us we were almost completely unemployable, but eventually Sullivan found a part-time job in a comic shop, which helped us to keep body and soul together. After signing on all summer I found work as a junior in a tattooist's on a quiet back street off the Leeds Road.

With my first pay cheque, I acquired a cheap ex-Army Land Rover from a guy that Sullivan knew at the comic shop. The lack of power steering meant it was totally impractical for day-to-day driving in town and it rattled horribly once you went above forty, but I'd fallen in love with it. Sullivan on the other hand took the piss and referred to it – albeit not without affection – as The Wreck of the Hesperus, although he was the first to admit that it came in handy for moving the band's guitars and amps around Bradford.

We still lived in the basement flat in West Bowling and we were young, skint and in love. Life was good.

Bradford Telegraph & Argus

13 July 1991

What's On – Music

Alternative rock night, with DJs and live music from Bradford's very own Sydenham Poyntz. Friday 20 July, 9pm til late at the Beehive, Westgate, Bradford.

£3 / £2 (NUS & unwaged).

"Bee" There or "Bee" Square!

Chapter Two

July 1991

Early on a Saturday morning I was woken up by the doorbell. It rang twice before I was fully awake: it had been a long night thanks to a late Sydenham Poyntz gig and we hadn't got home until gone two. Sullivan didn't as much as stir.

'Must be the postman,' I thought as I pulled on last night's dress and went to answer the door, but it wasn't the postman: it was Billy. He was clutching a sports bag and looked as if he'd been out all night.

'Oh, hello. Where on earth did you come from?' I said.

'Got the coach,' he mumbled.

'Why?'

He shrugged and stared at the ground. 'Nothing, I just fancied coming to see you.'

'What's up?'

His lower lip wobbled. 'Me and mum had a fight,' he said. 'And she grounded me and it's not fair and I hate her and I've come to stay with you.'

'Oh, fair enough. You'd better come in then.'

Billy dumped his bag on the sofa. 'Thanks.'

'What did you fight with your mum about?'

'I wanted to go to an all-night gig in Manchester with some mates but she wouldn't let me.'

'OK. We can talk about it later. You know where everything is, make yourself at home.'

I went back to the bedroom. 'Wake up,' I said to Sullivan, pushing on his shoulder. 'Billy's here, he says he's had a row with your mum.'

Sullivan sat up, yawned and rubbed his eyes. 'What? What time is it?'

'Seven o'clock. He said he got the coach.'

'Has he? Yeah, he can stay here if he wants.'

'But we've both got work today, we can't leave him here.'

'He'll be fine. Give him a day or two to get over himself, yeah?'

'Aren't you going to let your mum know?'

'Later.' He rolled over and went back to sleep.

There was no point in arguing so I shooed Billy into the kitchen to make tea and I phoned Barbara to let her know that he had turned up on our doorstep.

Barbara told me she was about to call us for the same reason, having discovered that Billy was missing not ten minutes previously when she'd got up for work. Her first thought was that he might have come to Bradford.

She confided to me that she didn't know what to do with him now he was sixteen and wouldn't do as he was told, and how it was doubly hard what with her being on her own. We agreed that it was probably best for everyone if Billy stayed with us for the rest of the weekend.

It was a busy day at work with four walk-in clients on top of the ones who'd already booked; Gary and I had hardly sat down all day and I'd barely had time to eat lunch, let alone think about Billy.

I was the first one to get home from work. I felt shattered and was looking forward to a cup of tea and maybe even a nap before we went out to that night's gig at The White Lion.

'Hiya,' I called as I opened the front door but there was no reply. The flat was deafeningly silent and smelled of weed.

Billy was sprawled face down on the sofa with one arm trailing on the floor and his T-shirt was rucked up, showing the pale, freckled skin of his back. The stash tin that I kept in the kitchen drawer was on the floor. Grass spilled out of the ziplock bag, the pouch of tobacco lay open and rolling papers were strewn over a Faith No More album. The bottle of Smirnoff that Sullivan kept in the freezer was lying uncapped and empty in the middle of the room.

'Oh, Billy. What the bloody hell have you done?'

He groaned.

I rushed over to him. 'Are you OK?'

Billy sighed and mumbled something I couldn't quite hear. *At least he hasn't been sick*, I thought as I went to the kitchen and poured a pint of water. Sullivan arrived home as I was rummaging in the cupboard for some aspirins.

'Christ. What's going on here?'

'Looks like your brother found my stash and your vodka.'

'You fucking idiot,' said Sullivan. He shook Billy awake.

Billy struggled to sit up and could hardly open his eyes. 'You don't care either,' he slurred. 'You, her, mum, you don't care. 'snot fair.'

'Shut up, Billy.'

'Why? You gonna hit me then, like you hit that bloke?'

'Don't be stupid.'

Billy's comment confused me. I put the tablets on the floor and handed him the glass. 'Here love, have this. It'll make you feel better.'

He squinted and swallowed half a pint of water.

'We can't leave him,' I said. 'What if he's ill or something?'

'He'll be fine,' said Sullivan. 'Are you going to behave yourself, our kid?'

'Yeah.' Billy groaned again and slumped back down on the sofa as we loaded the Wreck up with Sullivan's guitar and amp. We left him on the sofa, looking pale and wretched, when we drove to Rob's to pick him up for the gig.

Billy was fast asleep when we got home at half past midnight.

'What did Billy mean?' I said to Sullivan. We were lying spooned together in bed and moonlight shone through the thin curtains.

'What?'

'When he thought you were going to hit him, for getting wasted.'

'Oh, that. Nothing.'

'Nothing?' I rolled over to look at him in the dark.

'I've got a record,' he said after a long pause.

'You've got a *what*?'

He sighed, sat up and ran his fingers through his hair. 'A police record. Before I met you – it was not long after dad died – I was in a pub back home with some mates from school, and these three guys started on us for no reason at all. I punched one of them and got done for ABH, it went to court and I got a fine.'

'Oh, I see,' I said but I didn't see at all.

'Well?'

'Well, obviously violence is wrong; it's never the solution. But – I suppose if you were provoked then I guess that makes it different.'

'Extenuating circumstances, that's what the magistrate said. It's why I only got a fine and didn't get banged up.'

'Hey, it's OK,' I said. 'I love you.'

I couldn't imagine Sullivan ever being goaded to the point of lashing out and I pushed the thought away. After three years together I was certain I knew everything about him.

Bradford Telegraph & Argus

28 August 1992

What's On – Music

Friday 4th September at 9pm at The Windmill, 162 High Street, Bradford. Sydenham Poyntz with special guests The Chemistry Set.

FREE ENTRY!

Drinks 50p a shot/99p a pint all night.

Chapter Three

September 1992

Rob threw a birthday party in the cavernous house that he shared with five other postgraduates. The living room was wall-to-wall with people and a guy with a yellow Mohican and lilac dungarees was working the decks; The Pixies segued into My Bloody Valentine and the smoke from a dozen joints perfumed the air. It was a mild evening and someone had taken the sofa and chairs out the back to turn the weed-filled yard into an extra room.

We picked our way around the clumps of people and found a space for ourselves on the sticky carpet. Rob joined us and we toasted his birthday with cheap wine in chipped mugs.

A middle-aged woman in beads, a green kaftan and sensible sandals was reading the hand of a teenage girl who sat at her side. The older woman looked out of place amongst the students half her age and I wondered if she was someone's eccentric relative.

Rob noticed me looking. 'She's amazing,' he said.

'Who is she?'

He leaned in conspiratorially and scratched his straggly beard. 'That,' he said, 'is Maggie. She sells what is very probably the best gear in Bradford. And, if that wasn't enough, she's a freakishly good psychic too.'

Someone I didn't know tapped Rob on the shoulder and he stood up, passed me the last of his joint and wandered off.

'Dare you,' said Sullivan.

'I will if you will.'

'You're on.'

Maggie took my right hand in both of hers.

'You're artistic,' she said as she looked at my fingers. She had a soft Yorkshire accent and I had to lean in to hear her over the babble of the party.

'Yeah, that's right. I'm a tattooist in a place in town.'

She rubbed her thumb gently over my fingernails; it felt oddly sensual.

'Mmm. You're sensitive, but you can be stubborn sometimes, and you like to make plans, to be organised.'

'No way! You can tell all that by looking at my hand? I don't believe it.'

'It's a gift, pet. Palms, tarot, crystals – I do them all,' she said.

She tucked a greying curl of hair behind her ear and pointed at my palm with a blunt finger.

'I see some money here. A lot of money, but it will come with sadness too; do you see these little knots on the lifeline?'

I looked at my palm but the lines and creases were meaningless.

'Oh...How's that then? Do you mean an inheritance when someone's died?' I wondered who she could mean; there was no-one that I could think of who might leave me money.

'It could be, could be. It will be a force for good in the end, but it won't be without its challenges.'

'What do you mean? What sort of challenges?'

'You can either let things be the making of you, or let them break you.'

'I don't understand?'

Maggie looked at me and raised an eyebrow. There was something in her hooded hazel stare that made me think of tigers. I shivered and an icy feeling crept around my heart.

'The only way to make sense of change is to jump in and join the dance.'

'Oh.'

'Do you have children?'

I shook my head. 'No.'

'Do you see these?' She gestured at the base of my little finger, to a network of tiny lines where it joined my palm.

'Yes...?'

'You're going to have a baby,' she said.

'A baby? When?' I glanced at Sullivan and he looked back with an expression that might have been fright.

Maggie smiled. 'Oh, soon enough.'

'Are you sure? We...I...we're not planning to have a family.'

I tried to catch Sullivan's eye again but he wouldn't meet my gaze.

'No doubt about it, pet.' She smiled, folded my hand up like a flower and patted it closed.

Maggie turned to Sullivan. 'I can do you a reading too, if you'd like?'

He put his hands in his pockets. 'No, it's OK, but thanks. I don't believe in any of that psychic stuff.'

She laughed a wheezy smoker's laugh. 'Don't worry, I don't bite. But if you change your mind, come and see me some time. I've got a shop near the Oastler market.'

She dug in her beaded purse and took out a silver business card decorated with moons and stars in cherry-coloured ink. It advertised palmistry, tarot and crystal scrying by Magenta.

'Here you are. Pop in sometime when you're passing.'

I took the card and put it in my pocket for a reason I couldn't explain.

'Do you want kids?' I said to Sullivan as we walked home. It was two in the morning and a heavy fog hung over the city, muting the street lamps into Impressionist sunsets.

'Never really thought about it.'

'Me neither, I'm not even sure I want children. I mean, can you see the two of us, married with kids? It doesn't feel right.'

'Yeah, I know what you mean. Did you believe what she said? She was really vague, and a lot of it was obvious – everyone's got an artistic streak, haven't they?'

'I don't know...some of the things she said were pretty spot on. There has to be some truth in it, surely?'

'You are most *definitely* stubborn.'

'No I'm not.'

He laughed. 'Yes you are.'

I put my arm in his. 'Whatever. So we have a kid, inherit some money and have all sorts of stress because of it? That's a weird thing to say.'

'Fair enough.'

'Maybe we'll have seven,' I grinned. 'Like The Waltons. Can you imagine?'

He pulled a face. 'No.'

'A boy first, I'd name him after you.'

'Sullivan Sullivan?'

'Jeremy.'

'No way. I mean it.'

'What's your middle name?'

'Edward, after my grandpa. But don't tell anyone.'

'So...Edward, then Julianne, it's much nicer than Julia, then – oh, I don't know. What about Estella, Herbert, Jacob...and Ebenezer?'

'No, they're all too old-fashioned. Jimi. Marley. Django. Janis. Ringo.'

'*Ringo Sullivan*? You're crazy.'

We both laughed and he turned to kiss me, but at that moment a car sped pass, blaring music. A young lad was hanging out of the rear window and he roared something that was quickly lost in the fog. I was tired, slightly stoned and drunk; the noise made me jump and I suddenly felt panicky and frayed around the edges.

'She's only Rob's dealer, isn't she? I bet it's all a front, her party trick.'

'Party trick or not, that was some good gear that she had,' said Sullivan. 'I'm going to get her number off Rob.'

'It's your turn to go and score,' Sullivan said to me a week later.

'I bought the gear last time, *and* I've only got a tenner to last till Friday.'

'But I'm skint.'

'No you're not. You got paid yesterday.'

Sullivan harrumphed and took fifteen pounds from his jeans pocket.

'Here you go.'

'It's your turn still.'

'I'm busy.'

'You mean you don't want to go and see Maggie.'

'She's really weird.'

'She's Rob's mate, you should go.'

'He used to work with her in the off-licence; he said she's a proper witch and she casts spells and everything.' Sullivan pulled a face.

'No she's not.'

'She gives me the creeps. I'll go next time, alright?'

'OK.' I sighed and picked up the phone.

Maggie lived in a house overlooking a patch of waste ground behind the football club. It was decorated with Indian bedspreads on the walls and a garish plaster statuette of the Virgin Mary peered out from behind sticks of incense on a dresser covered in knick-knacks. Clots of blue and red candle wax formed alien silhouettes over a dusty wine bottle.

Maggie saw me looking at the statue as she bustled around the kitchenette with the tea things.

'Do you like her? I picked her up in Goa.'

'She's...certainly different. Do you travel a lot?'

'Oh, I've been all over. I travelled overland halfway round India and back, and I once spent a year living in a commune in Morocco. The tales I could tell you.'

'Really? It sounds fascinating.'

'Oh, another time pet, another time.'

A Dachshund was curled up asleep in the only armchair and showed no sign of moving so I sat down on a velvet beanbag instead. Once the tea was ready Maggie produced a slab of hash the size of a chocolate bar from a tangle of scarves in her dresser. She unwrapped it and cut off a piece with a penknife.

'Your young man isn't with you today?' said Maggie as she weighed the eighth on a set of old-fashioned brass scales. It balanced perfectly first time and she dabbed up the crumbs with the tip of her index finger and put them into a tiny plastic bag with the rest. She wrapped the block back up in its cling film and scarf and buried it once more in the drawer.

'Sullivan? No – he's a bit busy at the moment; he's got a lot on at work. You know how it is.'

'You mean he's still afraid that I'll try and tell his fortune?' she said.

I laughed. 'How did you guess?'

'Oh, you don't need to be a psychic to tell that.'

We drank our tea and smoked a companionable joint, and I wondered what on earth she meant.

Bradford Telegraph & Argus
15 February 1993
Sydenham Poyntz at the Tyersal Community Centre, Bradford

As a self-proclaimed fan of rock music, the news that local band Sydenham Poytnz were playing a headline show on Valentine's Day filled me with anticipation.

Well known for locally for intimate gigs on the Bradford pub circuit, Sydenham Poyntz have at long last garnered enough of a following amongst their fans to headline at the 150-capacity Tyersal Community Centre.

As well as their lesser-known original material, including a heart-wrenching ballad or two, the band gave a unique twist to classic 1960s and 1970s hard-rock favourites that had the appreciative audience all fired up by the end of the evening.

Chapter Four

August–October 1993

It was my day off and I was lying on the sofa watching *Neighbours* when the phone rang.

'Hello?'

'I've passed!' shouted Billy. 'Two Bs and a C!'

'Oh my God, well done, that's fantastic news!'

'I know, I really thought I was gonna fail…mum can't believe it…here, do you reckon they're good enough to get into uni?'

'I'll say. Get on the phone to Clearing, see what you can find.'

'Maybe they can get me on a course at Bradford? Do you think so?'

'Well, give them a call, but be quick before all the places go.'

'Will do! You're amazing!'

'Billy called,' I said to Sullivan when he got home from work.

'I know – mum rang me at the shop to tell me the good news. We're both gobsmacked that he did it.'

Sullivan phoned home as soon as it turned six o'clock and Billy told him that he had already been accepted onto a

Computer Science degree at Bradford, and thanks to the university accommodation office he had been set up with a room in a shared house out in Baildon.

Sullivan offered that Billy could stay at the flat, but he was adamant that he would live in the house that the university had found for him; I sensed he was trying to prove that he could take care of himself. Billy mentioned he would look for a part-time job as well once he'd settled in.

'You could work for Sydenham Poyntz as a roadie,' joked Sullivan. 'I might even throw in a few guitar lessons, too.'

Three weeks into his first term, Billy invited us to Baildon. 'Make a weekend of it,' he said on the phone. 'Come over on Saturday night, and we'll go out for a few drinks. You can crash over if you like.'

For once Sullivan had no gigs booked so once I'd finished work I drove the Wreck out to Baildon on a bitterly cold October afternoon. I scored an eighth from Maggie and Sullivan got a bottle of supermarket Scotch as a housewarming present.

It was the first time that we had been to Billy's new place; he had refused our offers of help with the move and instead Barbara had driven up from Salford with Billy's belongings in the back of her Austin Allegro and his bicycle strapped to the roof-rack. She'd described the house to us as being in a quiet area.

She wasn't joking. We followed Billy's instructions and drove through Bradford, north over the river, through Baildon and out the other side. I was certain we'd taken a wrong turning when we arrived in the middle of nowhere with the moors spread out beneath us in the dusk like a great patchwork quilt, but Sullivan checked the directions again and told me to take left turn past the golf course and then another left down a rutted narrow track. At last we came to a small, two-storey farmhouse with weathered russet bricks and a sagging roof. It looked like something out of Wuthering Heights.

'Is this it?' The farmhouse was the only building in sight.

'Must be,' said Sullivan. I parked the Wreck and he strode off and knocked on the door.

We were in the right place after all.

'Come in,' said Billy. 'This is the kitchen.'

He showed us a room with a tiled floor, a butler sink, an enormous black range and a solid wooden table that would have easily seated twelve.

'We live in here mainly; the Aga's always on and keeps it warm.'

We saw the parlour too; it had a faded red sofa and an ornately patterned carpet: a hundred years ago it would have been the room saved for best and never used except when important visitors came. It looked the same now.

'And there's the two bedrooms,' he continued. 'But Tina's asleep and Rudy's not around.'

'Tina?' said Sullivan.

Billy blushed. 'Tina's my...well, she's my girlfriend. We've been seeing each other a couple of weeks now.'

'Look forward to meeting her, our kid,' said Sullivan. 'And Rudy's the guy you share with, right?'

'Right. He's out at the moment.'

A teenage girl came down the stairs and draped herself over the newel post. Billy put his arm around her waist and introduced us.

'Tina, this is my brother Sullivan, and this is Sullivan's girlfriend Julia. Sullivan, Julia, this is Tina.'

'Pleased to meet you,' I said.

'Hi,' Tina said, peering with ratty, mascara'd eyes through a curtain of pale hair. She picked at her nails and looked bored.

'So how did you two meet?' asked Sullivan.

'Tina's a student nurse,' said Billy before she had a chance to reply. 'We met in the union bar on campus.'

I must be getting old, I thought. She looked about fourteen.

That evening we all walked into Baildon village to the pub and Rudy joined us too. He turned out to be a big, tall guy with short hair and wire-rimmed glasses.

'So Rudy, what are you studying?' I asked him as we drank our pints.

He stared at me for a good five seconds before replying. He smirked and licked his lips until I blushed and looked away.

'Now, why would you want to know a thing like that?' he said and smirked some more until I felt so awkward I turned around and talked to Billy and Tina instead.

Tina was immature and whiny; clearly she adored Billy but she clung to him all night like a shipwrecked sailor and it was all I could do to have a conversation with him. She held his hand constantly, sat on his lap and kissed him in front of us all: everything about her screamed insecurity. She followed him to the bar when he bought a round of drinks and I was surprised she didn't follow him to the toilet as well.

After an uncomfortable hour, Sullivan and I made our excuses and went to play pool.

'Student nurse, my arse,' said Sullivan once we'd reached the safety of the table. 'No way is she eighteen.'

'Thank God for that, I thought it was me. She can't be a day over fifteen.'

'I'll have a word later,' he said and potted two reds off the break.

Q Magazine

September 1994

Honesty – Sydenham Poyntz

Debut by Bradford rock god sensations-in-waiting. Warning: may contain traces of 60s sci-fi.

For all the Britpop hubble and bubble in the charts, there's always room for straight up 4/4 rock and roll and this debut by Sydenham Poyntz is a blistering record packed with gems honed by years slogging on the local gig circuit.

From the vision of a terrifying capitalist dystopia conjured up in *Rainy Days,* the opening twang, emotive lyrics and lush acoustic soundscapes of *Weird Brotherhood* and the raw, drum-led version of the *Joe 90* theme – which is guaranteed to have you humming it for weeks – Sydenham Poyntz have proved that they can punch well above their weight.

●●●●○

Chapter Five

October 1993

At closing time we walked back to the farmhouse, up a winding lane over the moors, through a creaking wooden gate and past gravelly spoil heaps. There were no lights for miles around and the moors were silent. The farmhouse seemed more remote than ever in the dark.

We sat in the kitchen in the warmth of the Aga and Sullivan produced the whisky and I rolled a couple of joints to pass around. Tina took a mouthful of Scotch but pulled a face like a cat taking medicine.

'Ewww,' she said. 'Is it meant to taste like that?'

Billy rushed to the fridge and got a bottle of Coke. He topped her drink up but the rest of us had to go without.

We put on a Young Ones video and Sullivan, Billy and I all had a fit of hysterical giggles when Vyvyan lost his head and the three of us sang along to Motorhead at the tops of our voices, but Tina sat there drinking her whisky and Coke, smoking and looking blank. Rudy laughed at strange moments, as if he had another TV programme playing in his head that only he could see.

Between the drinks and the joints, I was feeling pleasantly mellow when suddenly Tina leapt up on wobbly Bambi legs and hiccupped that she was going to be sick. She barely made it to the bathroom in time.

Poor kid, she looked as pale as milk and it sounded as though she was being turned inside out. Billy rushed to be with her and ten minutes later they both emerged: Tina shivering in Billy's arms, with dripping hair and smeared mascara.

'Sorry guys…I need to take her to bed,' said Billy.

'I'll give you a hand,' said Sullivan.

He passed the joint to me before he helped Billy carry Tina upstairs. The video had finished and the screen was just grey snow but Rudy didn't move from his chair. There was something about him that made me feel uneasy so I handed the joint to him at arm's length and followed the others upstairs.

Tina lay passed out on the bed where Billy and Sullivan had left her; they were faffing about what to do next so I shooed them away to give her some privacy. Her jeans and top were soaking wet so I undressed her; as I peeled off the cheap, thin material I was surprised to see that her legs and body were covered in red bites. I'd seen something like that once before on a lad at uni who'd made the mistake of buying a second-hand mattress. They were bed-bug bites – something that belonged in Dickensian squalor, not in late twentieth century Bradford. I wondered where she lived, and what sort of parents would let their daughter sleep in an infested bed.

I rolled Tina onto her side so she wouldn't choke if she vomited again in her sleep and covered her with the duvet. Once that was done I stumbled downstairs and scrubbed my hands in the kitchen sink. I itched all over.

'Are you alright?' said Sullivan.

'Just tired.' I furtively scratched my arms. 'Think I might call it a night.'

'You can sleep in the parlour if you want,' Billy said, and we traipsed out to the Wreck to get our things.

Sullivan and I laid out our sleeping bags in the freezing front room and it was so cold my teeth were chattering before we'd finished. There was a gas fire at the far end of the room and I lit it with my Zippo. Sooty flames leapt up and the room immediately filled with the smell of scorched dust, but it was better than the prospect of hypothermia. We crawled into our sleeping bags fully dressed and were asleep in moments.

I woke up in the middle of the night; sweating, groggy and confused. The room was like a sauna, my mouth was parched dry and I had a raging headache. I turned off the fire, stripped off my jeans and socks and fanned myself, but I needed some water and so I tiptoed to the kitchen. The heavy parlour door creaked and Sullivan muttered something in his sleep that I didn't catch. A light was on somewhere in the house, which was lucky because I didn't want to try and find my way around in the dark.

Rudy was in the kitchen watching the TV with the sound turned down; the fug of smoke told me he had smoked several more joints after we'd gone to bed. As I walked into the kitchen I realised he was watching a porn video and I instantly felt uncomfortable: I was only wearing a T-shirt and underwear.

'Excuse me,' I said and hurried to the sink. Rudy said nothing and continued to stare at the television.

I took a mug from the draining board and turned on the cold tap; the pipes thumped and banged like Vulcan's forge. I didn't hear Rudy when he crept up behind me.

He slammed his hand against my right breast and his other hand was on my thigh; his fingers curled into my underwear. I smelled his sweat and heard his ragged breath barely an inch from my ear.

I tried to wriggle away but he held me even more tightly; the hand on my breast gripped and squeezed harder as he roughly jabbed his fingers in an attempt to get inside me. I could feel his erection pressing into the small of my back. Time solidified and I thought I was going to die.

'You know you want me,' he panted. 'That's why you're here.'

He licked my cheek. His saliva ran down my face and his breath was hot and rank with tobacco and whisky.

I tried to scream but all that came out was a useless whimper. Rudy took his hand off my breast and clamped it over my mouth to muffle me. His thumb jabbed against my nose and suddenly I couldn't breathe. I tried to fight but it was useless – he had pushed me hard against the sink and was using his weight to stop me from breaking free.

Terror turned to a blind red rage and some deep-rooted need for survival kicked in. I screamed again despite his hand over my face; I was furious now, and I struggled harder, trying to make contact and hit him anywhere, in any way I could. Hair flew into my eyes as we fought and I finally hit him in the chest with my elbow. He relaxed his grip for half a moment and I lashed out and kicked him in the kneecap. There was a crunch like breaking wood and Rudy howled. He staggered sideways; his hand caught in the leg of my underwear and I fell against the sink as he collapsed, clutching his ruined knee.

The mug crashed from my hand and smashed on the flagstoned floor. As Rudy fell he hit his head on the side of the Aga and he slumped to the ground. His glasses spun off and clattered under the table. I screamed.

I burst into tears as Sullivan appeared at the kitchen door.

'What the fuck?'

'He tried...oh God...' I sobbed. 'I...I'd come to get some water, he grabbed me and I hit him and...and...' I gestured at Rudy lying on the floor and forced myself to look at him. There was something wrong that my panicked brain couldn't work out.

'I heard you shouting. Are you alright?'

No, I'm not bloody well alright, I wanted to say. *He tried to rape me, and you're asking if I'm alright.*

I gulped my tears back and took a deep breath. 'Yeah. Think so.'

He gave me a brief hug and knelt at Rudy's side

'Rudy, get up!' He shook Rudy but he lay, unmoving, on the kitchen floor.

My breath came in heaving gasps as I watched them.

'Rudy! Get up!'

Sullivan looked at Rudy and then at me. 'Fucking hell, Julia.' He sounded flat and dull. 'You've gone and fucking killed him.'

I ran to the kitchen sink and vomited. I turned the taps full on and screamed again. This didn't feel real: it was as if I was looking at myself from a distance; detached and suddenly untethered from everything that was going on. All I could think about was that Sullivan must be wrong – he *had* to be wrong – Rudy couldn't be dead. I was furious. He'd made a mistake, he'd lied to me; I couldn't have killed him. I wanted to wake up.

Sullivan wrapped his arms around me and I buried my face in his chest, but my screams brought Billy running downstairs. He was wild-eyed and was still fastening his jeans as he ran into the kitchen. He flicked the light switch and the fluorescent tubes crackled like lightning and exposed every detail of what I'd done.

'Jesus, what's happened?' He looked at Sullivan, at me, and back to Sullivan. His eyes grew wider and wider as he saw Rudy lying on the floor, the mug shattered into bits and me with my puffy, tear-streaked face. Billy's freckles stood out on his pale skin like splashes of blood.

'Sit down,' said Sullivan. 'Where's Tina?'

'Asleep,' Billy said. 'Why?'

'Good. We've got a situation,' Sullivan said in that same flat, dead voice.

'Rudy...he was going to rape me – and I hit him and...'

The tears came back and I couldn't say any more. My legs gave way and I half sat and half collapsed onto the kitchen floor. The fluorescent light stung my eyes.

Billy's mouth opened and shut like a goldfish's. 'R–R–Rudy would never do that – he's alright – I know he's a bit weird, but he wouldn't hurt anyone...Is he OK?'

'I can't find a pulse,' said Sullivan.

I started to shiver and wrapped my arms around my knees to try and make it stop.

'We've got to phone the ambulance!' said Billy.

'No, no, hang on a minute.' I wanted to cry but the tears wouldn't come. I sucked down a deep breath and tried to get my thoughts into some sort of order.

'If...if he's dead and we call the ambulance they'll get the police and they won't believe me. They'll do me for murder. Oh, fucking hell.'

'And we can't get the police involved because of Tina,' said Sullivan.

Billy had the good grace to look ashamed. 'How do you know?'

'Because she's about fourteen.'

'Actually she'll be sixteen at Christmas.'

'And she's not a student nurse?'

'She's still at school.'

Sullivan rubbed his eyes and picked up the Scotch from the kitchen table. He took a long drink and passed the bottle to me and I did the same: the raw whisky burned my throat until I coughed. The pain gave me focus and I suddenly realised I was still undressed.

'I need to put some clothes on.'

I got up from the floor and took the whisky with me to the parlour, where I ripped off my T-shirt and underwear. I imagined I could still smell Rudy's stench as I balled my dirty clothes up. I took some clean knickers from my bag, swallowed more whisky and got dressed – jeans, shirt, socks, boots, the lot. I needed to be covered up; hidden. I took another swig from the bottle before I could face going back.

Billy looked ghostly and wraithlike in the harsh glare of the kitchen light. I leant over the sink and scrubbed my hands and face with washing up liquid and a dishcloth until they were red: I felt filthy and needed a bath.

'What do we do?' pleaded Billy, on the brink of tears.

'We have to make it look like an accident. Like Julia said, the police won't believe the truth,' said Sullivan.

'What about putting him in there?' said Billy, pointing at the large chest freezer in the corner.

'No,' said Sullivan. 'You'd only do that if you had something to hide.'

I pulled out a chair and sat at the table. 'What…what do you mean "an accident"?'

'We have to take him outside, not here: we don't want the police poking round. How about on the moors somewhere?'

'There are some tools in the shed,' said Billy. 'You could cut him up...'

'No! Nobody is cutting anybody up!'

I made myself look at Rudy, at his head at an awkward angle and with a lump behind his ear, the pale blue check of his shirt against the dark tiles and his skin turned waxy by the blazing kitchen light. *Cut him up*? Jesus, the thought of it made me feel sick – even after what he'd done Rudy didn't deserve to be hacked up like a piece of meat. I drank some more whisky and tried to shake the image from my mind.

'There's old mine workings all over the moors,' said Sullivan. 'If Rudy had gone for a walk late at night, got lost and fallen down one of them…'

'Where?'

'There are abandoned mines all over Baildon Moor – and the old holding tank, it's nothing but a hole in the ground now – we could take him in the Wreck and put him down that. Nobody would ever find him.'

'You take him,' I said. 'I can't do it.'

'I can't drive,' said Sullivan. 'You know that.'

'Billy?'

He shook his head. 'Me neither.'

Chapter Six

October 1993

We argued for what seemed like hours about what to do. Billy and Sullivan couldn't agree whether Rudy's wallet should go with the body or be left in the house. Eventually we decided to put his house keys in his pocket (Billy did that; I couldn't bear to touch Rudy even now he was dead), but we left his wallet behind on the table. They dressed him in his parka and I forced myself to watch. It made me feel sick; his arms were limp and it took three or four goes to force each one into a sleeve.

'What about his shoes?' said Sullivan.

'What about them?'

'He's got bare feet; he wouldn't have gone out like that.'

Billy found Rudy's socks and baseball boots by the kitchen door. They took one foot each, rolled on the white towelling socks and pushed his feet into the boots. They struggled and eventually undid all the laces to get his flaccid feet to fit inside. By the time they finished Sullivan was grey and sweating and Billy was crying.

Once Rudy was dressed they lifted him up by holding one of his arms around each of their shoulders and walked him through the farmhouse and out the front to the Land Rover. His feet dragged on the stony ground and his head sagged obscenely with each step.

My teeth were chattering from a combination of exhaustion and cold. Billy and Sullivan put Rudy in the rear seat and buckled the belt to stop him from slipping off. With his head slumped sideways he looked like he was drunk.

'I'll stay here,' said Billy. 'In case Tina wakes up.'

'No,' I said. 'We need your help...at the other end.'

'No,' said Sullivan. 'You wait here, we can manage the rest.'

Billy visibly sagged with relief.

'But I can't carry him!' I said. 'I need both of you to help.'

'We'll manage,' said Sullivan. 'We'll have to.'

'What if someone sees us?'

'It's the middle of the night. They won't.'

Billy went inside and I started the car. I was still shivering but Sullivan didn't seem to notice; he didn't speak except to give me instructions – *drive down the track; now go down this footpath; pull in here*. The Wreck rattled across uneven moorland at four miles an hour. I parked in the lee of a hill and switched off the engine.

'There's the abandoned mine over there,' said Sullivan. He pointed left, to something invisible in the gloom. 'Turn off the lights, let your eyes adjust. We'll put Rudy in there, OK?'

I did as I was told: I hadn't got the strength to argue. I got out of the car and unbuckled Rudy's seatbelt. He lolled to one side but I tried not to touch him – the thought of his dead flesh against mine made me retch. I was shivering uncontrollably again now that I wasn't concentrating on driving.

The first pink fingers of sunrise tentatively reached over the horizon but it did nothing to dispel the eeriness of the moor. A sheep bleated, making me jump; my skin crept as adrenalin flooded through my body.

'Right,' said Sullivan. I thought his nerves must have been made of steel.

'You saw what Billy and I did earlier? I'll take one arm, you take the other one and we'll walk him. It's about fifty yards down there.'

'I can't touch him.' Nausea rose in my throat and I gagged on the taste of bile and whisky.

'We haven't got a choice. Believe me, I'd rather not be doing this either but we've got a job to do. OK?'

I knew he was right. Sullivan pulled Rudy's body from the back of the Land Rover. *He can't hurt you now,* I said to myself as I gritted my teeth. I looped Rudy's right arm over my right shoulder and put my left arm under his. Sullivan took the opposite side and we half carried, half dragged Rudy across the moor.

Rudy's chin bounced against his chest. His arm felt rubbery and cold; he smelled stale and sour and was heavier than I had expected. I sagged under his weight and my back and shoulders quickly began to burn with the effort, but I bit my lip and struggled on. My eyes slowly adjusted to the darkness as we inched along but I still stumbled two or three times on the tussocky grass.

The abandoned mine was little more than a hole in the ground in a small copse. A stream babbled in the distance. There was an opening about two feet square in front of us that I could barely see in the dark.

'We're going to put him down there,' said Sullivan. We held Rudy's feet over the opening.

'Are you sure?'

'There isn't anywhere else.'

'One...two...three...'

We dropped him in. There was a splash and a muffled thump as he hit the bottom of the shaft a second or two later.

'It's not very deep.'

'It's the best we could do,' said Sullivan. He wiped his hands on his jeans and we walked back to the Wreck without speaking. The sun glowed pink on the horizon and the moors were covered with pale mist.

We drove back to the farmhouse, still in silence: I wanted to say something but every time I opened my mouth I stopped. Nothing seemed to be right.

Billy was pacing the kitchen when we returned.

'Have you...?' he asked.

'Yes,' said Sullivan. 'We...'

Billy sat down and clapped his hands over his ears, like a child. 'I don't want to know!'

I knelt at his side. 'Billy, I need a bath. I still feel filthy from when...from earlier.'

'Yeah, help yourself.'

I ran to the bathroom and locked the door. I filled the claw-footed tub with tepid water, and made a lather from the cracked green soap. I rinsed my hair too, but it made no difference; I felt as if I would never be clean again. I felt exposed and vulnerable lying naked in the bath so I quickly dried myself and dressed once more.

Back in the kitchen, Billy and Sullivan were sitting at the table with the whisky bottle between them. They looked like a pair of battle-weary soldiers; the tension had scored deep lines on their faces and darkened the hollows of their eyes with blue shadows.

'I want to go home,' I said to Sullivan. I needed to be back in our flat, far away from everything that had happened here tonight. I wanted to be safe my own bed and sleep for a week.

'Please don't go,' said Billy.

'Sullivan?' I said. 'I can't stay here.'

'Let's leave it a while, eh?' he said. 'We're not in any hurry.'

Defeated, I pretended it didn't matter and filled the kettle to make some tea. As I stood by the sink I noticed something under the table.

'We forgot about Rudy's glasses,' I said. I went to pick them up.

'Don't do that,' he said. 'You'll leave fingerprints.'

He took a cloth from the worktop and used that to lift them up. He put the cracked glasses next to the wallet on the kitchen table, and covered them with the dishcloth.

'Now what? What are we going to do with those?'

'I'll think of something,' said Sullivan and lapsed back into silence.

I made three mugs of tea – splashing milk on the kitchen worktop because I was shaking so badly – and we sat in the kitchen without speaking, each of us lost in our own thoughts.

Tina appeared as we were drinking our tea.

'Wondered where you'd gone,' she said to Billy, who was sitting slumped over the table. She sat down next to him and tried to give him a cuddle but Billy didn't stir. She pouted.

'I'm starving,' she said. 'What's for breakfast?'

She opened the fridge but there was nothing in there, bar a tub of margarine and the carton of milk. She tried the cupboard instead and picked up a packet of cereal but the box was empty. As I watched her, I realised that I was ravenous too.

'Can't you go to the shop? I'm hungry and there's nowt to eat.'

'In a minute. Can't face it right now,' he mumbled.

Tina sulked. 'Why can't you face it? I'm hungry.'

'I feel like shit, don't want to go out.'

'I think he's coming down with the flu,' said Sullivan.

To be fair Billy looked the part with his drawn face and the dark pouches under his eyes.

'I'll go,' I said with fake brightness: at least it would get me out of the house for a few minutes to clear my head.

'Thanks,' said Sullivan. 'I'll come with you; we'll leave the patient with Nurse Tina.'

I drove aimlessly around Baildon; I couldn't think or concentrate. We eventually found a Spar and I bought a box of cornflakes, some bacon, six eggs, a white sliced loaf and more milk. Sullivan added another half-bottle of Scotch to the basket.

'We can't afford it,' I said. 'Put it back.'

'I need it.'

'The rent's due next week, we're short as it is.'

'Sod the rent.'

I left the whisky in the basket.

I was convinced that the shopkeeper – an elderly man in a grey pullover and purple turban – could tell that there was something wrong with me, some sort of mark of Cain on my forehead. I did my best to arrange my face into a smile, but my hands began to shake again as I tried to put the shopping into the flimsy plastic bag: Sullivan had to finish packing. I wanted to shout out, confess to what I'd done, but instead I fumbled for my purse and paid, my numb fingers spilling coins onto the counter.

I could barely get the key in the ignition. Sullivan opened the whisky and passed me the uncapped bottle; I took a long swallow before I could start the engine.

Billy was hunched at the kitchen table with his head in his hands but Tina was a raging whirlwind.

'What did you have to tell them for?' she yelled. Flecks of spit flew from her mouth.

Sullivan strode in and positioned himself between them.

'Nobody told anyone anything,' he said quietly. 'We figured it out for ourselves, you're only fifteen and it shows.'

'Fuck off,' she shouted and stormed upstairs.

'Make her go away,' said Billy. 'She's doing my head in.'

I went upstairs. Tina was face down on Billy's bed, crying.

'Come on, love,' I said. 'Billy's not well, he needs to rest, get some peace and quiet. Why don't you pop home and leave him with us?'

'No.'

'Why, what's the matter?'

She turned over and sniffed. 'Billy's not got the flu, he's been right weird ever since you lot turned up. He's going to dump me, isn't he?'

I sighed. 'No, that's not true. Billy's ill; you saw the state he was in. Why don't we let him go to bed and have a proper sleep?'

'Don't want to go home.'

'Why's that?'

She shrugged.

'I'll give you a lift. Where do you live?'

'Buttershaw Estate.'

'Fine, get your stuff together.'

The journey there and back took nearly an hour: guilt made me drive under the speed limit all the way. I tried not to think about Rudy but I felt sick and couldn't concentrate properly: once I almost drove through a red light and I kept checking the rear-view mirror for police cars.

'How's school?' I asked Tina.

She shrugged. 'I'm not going any more.'

'Why's that?'

'I was always getting in trouble for being late, and there's no point doing exams. I'll leave soon as I'm sixteen.'

'What do you want to do when you leave?'

'You ask a lot of questions, don't you?'

I turned on the radio and anonymous pop music filled the car.

Tina directed me to an estate on the outskirts of the city. Ranks of grey houses surrounded a square of cratered turf in a mockery of the traditional village green; a slashed mattress and the remains of a burned-out car lay in the centre of the grass. A woman pushed a pram across the road.

'Drop us off here, will you? Dad'll give me a hiding if he thinks I've been out all night.'

I pulled the Wreck into a parking space outside a minimart with metal grilles over the windows.

'Your dad hits you?'

She shrugged. 'He's not my real dad. He's mum's boyfriend, he hates us kids.'

'But that's awful! Does your mum know?'

Tina laughed a grim and mirthless bark. 'What the fuck would you know about my Mum?'

'Have you got someone you could talk to? A teacher, maybe?'

'Teachers? You're joking; they'd only call the social.'

Q Magazine

January 1995

Q&A: The Sydenham Poyntz Interview

Sydenham Poyntz must surely be the biggest thing to come out of Bradford in recent years. Their first album sold 60,000 copies in the first month following its release last summer, and in December the band embarked on their first headlining tour across the UK and Europe. *Q* caught up with lead singer Sullivan in London between gigs.

How the devil are you?

Good, thanks. Yourself?

Very well, thanks for asking. What are you drinking?

Thanks. Builder's tea please, milk and no sugar.

That's not very rock n' roll, is it?

(Laughs). No, it isn't. I've got a bit of a hangover, a cuppa will sort me right out. It was a late one last night; we were up until six this morning, celebrating...

You've gone from playing pubs to headlining at the Brixton Academy last night. That's quite a journey, how did you manage that?

It's unreal, you know? Two years ago we were playing gigs to fifty people in local clubs, and now this. It's like a dream being on stage at Brixton playing to thousands of people. Next stop Wembley Arena! Actually we're playing Leeds next week so in some regards we haven't gone far at all.

Let's talk about your status as an overnight success.

"Overnight success?" *(Laughs)*. We've been going for seven years! The four of us met at university and started jamming together straight away. We hit it off immediately – we're all very much on the same wavelength. In a very 1980s student way we named ourselves after Sydenham Poytnz who was this revolutionary guy, a commander in the English Civil War who fought against the King. We saw ourselves as some sort of revolutionaries too, trying to use the forces of music to change the world.

It was only when we finally got some cash together and recorded a demo EP did we start to get noticed. Dave Rook on Radio 1 played it a lot and before you know it we've got a three-album deal.

How have things changed since the early days?

I don't like to think back on the past too much, you know? It's much better to look forward and focus on the future than look back and dwell on things.

Why's that?

(Pause). It's not something I feel comfortable thinking about. We are where we are. Next question...

We were talking about how the band has evolved.

Yeah. We're still making music and trying to change the world – and provide the record-buying public with an alternative to this whole Britpop thing that's going on. We've got better equipment now I guess; we used to have the crappiest amps and gear you could imagine. But no, apart from that we're a bunch of mates who hang out together and love music.

You've made a decision to include cover versions on this album but there is a lot of your own material too. How does it feel to be judged on songs you've written yourself?

When we first started we would only play cover versions, that whole 1970s rock vibe: Led Zep, Bad Company, you know? But we were doing original tracks back in '91, '92 – some really soppy ballads to begin with, I think those were Robbo's [*Rob Kelly, Sydenham Poyntz's drummer*] and then the other songs started to come together out of rehearsals and jams. But there's still a place for cover versions. I got into the whole Gerry Anderson 1960s sci-fi thing recently: Thunderbirds and puppets and that. We played the Joe 90 theme for a laugh once in a sound check and it went down so well it's our opening number now. Everyone thinks it's by Dr Feelgood. (Laughs).

Have you got far with the material for the new album?

The next album? Yeah, it's coming together nicely. We'll be back in the studio in January to lay down some tracks once we're done with the tour. We're working on ideas all the time and a couple of songs from the live set should make the cut. I'm into the idea of very snappy, three-minute tracks right now. Punchy rock numbers, no messing about, you know?

What are the themes in your music that chime with the audiences?

A lot of what we write about is the kind of thing everyone can relate to – getting drunk on a Friday night with your mates and realising your boring hometown isn't so bad after all. Fears about nuclear war and the apocalypse; fighting with your girlfriend and making up afterwards; working in a crappy job and dreaming about being on holiday – palm trees on the beach. They're all pretty universal themes.

Which is better – Blur or Oasis?

Neither, I don't get that Britpop thing at all. There are loads of bands out there right now that all sound the same, and everyone will have forgotten them this time next year. Everyone's trying to sound like The Kinks and The Jam twenty, thirty years too late.

Are you naming names?

No. I'm not into slagging off other people. All I'll say is Britpop's another example of disposable fashion – that whole band rivalry thing, like the Beatles and the Stones, yeah? It's all manufactured by the press. I always preferred The Who anyway. Keith Moon, I'd love to have him on drums.

Chapter Seven

October 1993

I drove back to Baildon just as slowly, focussing on the traffic and trying not to think. The last few hours seemed unreal, like a hangover from a bad dream: maybe if I drove home I'd find Sullivan still asleep in bed and that none of this had ever happened. Instead I turned left at the ring road and headed north.

Sullivan was in the kitchen, frowning and smoking a joint.

I put a hand on his shoulder and noticed he was shaking. 'Are you OK?'

'Yeah.'

We heard a motorbike driving up the path and then the doorbell rang. We looked at each other with rising panic.

'Is it the police?' I whispered.

'No – it can't be – can it?'

'Maybe it's someone for Billy?'

The bell rang again; two long rings that were followed by a series of knocks.

'Can you see who it is?'

'Not from here.'

'Rudy!' called a voice through the letterbox. 'Are you there, man?'

I sagged with relief. *Not the police,* I mouthed.

'I'll get it,' said Sullivan. 'Say he's gone out.'

I held my breath as he went to the door.

'I was looking for Rudy. Is he in?'

'Sorry, haven't seen him this morning,'

'Oh. Did he leave anything for me?'

Sullivan shrugged. 'I don't think so.'

'Did he say when he'd be back? Only it's important.'

'You'd better come in,' said Sullivan.

Don't let him in, he'll know what we've done, said the voice in my head, but the man walked into the kitchen. He had long hair and a goatee beard and was wearing bike leathers.

He sat down at the far end of the table, painfully close to the dishcloth that hid Rudy's belongings. My nerves began tingling and another wave of panic surged through me. I pushed my hands under the table to hide the fact my fists were clenched bone-white.

'Can we help?'

'Er, not sure. You two know Rudy, right?'

'Yeah, we're friends of his,' said Sullivan.

'I've not met you before, that's all. Can't be too careful, you know how it is.'

'Sure,' said Sullivan and offered him the joint.

'Cool. Thanks, man.' He took a deep toke and looked thoughtful. 'Thing is, Rudy's got a big order for me and I'll be in the shit if he doesn't deliver.' He fiddled with his earring.

'Oh. What sort of stuff?' said Sullivan.

The man passed the joint to me and picked a strand of tobacco from his bottom lip. 'Fifty trips,' he said. 'Got a bit of a thing going down tonight, Rudy promised he'd have the gear for me this morning.'

'Sorry,' said Sullivan. 'As soon as he comes back I'll let him know you've been.'

'Thanks,' said the man as he got up to leave. 'I appreciate it.'

We listened to the motorbike driving away.

'Fucking hell – fifty tabs?' I said. 'What's Rudy doing?'

'No idea. I don't know, maybe I've misunderstood something.'

'It doesn't sound like it?'

Sullivan looked around the kitchen.

'What have you lost?'

'I need to have a look in his room but I don't want to leave fingerprints.'

There was a box of disposable gloves in the Wreck that I'd been meaning to take to work all week. I brought the box back and we each struggled into a pair. Sullivan took Rudy's wallet from under the dishcloth and removed its contents one by one. It held the ephemera of a student's life: a laminated university library ticket, an NUS membership card with a stapled photo, a Midland Bank cash card and fifteen pounds in fivers. He lined the items up and put the money to one side.

'What shall we do with this?' I asked, gesturing at the things on the table. 'Burn them in the Aga?'

Sullivan replaced the cards and folded the wallet closed.

'No; why would a missing man burn his wallet? We'll put it in his bedroom and make it look like he went out.'

'But would Rudy have gone out without his glasses?'

'These are broken, right? Maybe he had a spare pair and he left these behind.'

He folded the notes into his jeans pocket and picked up Rudy's glasses and wallet.

'Where's Billy?' I asked.

'He was in a right state. I gave him some whisky and put him to bed.'

Rudy's room was a mess. The desk and the floor were covered in clothes and magazines; the curtains were closed and the gloomy room smelt of rotten things and socks. Judge Dredd glared at us from a poster on the wall.

Sullivan pulled open a drawer in the white melamine chest, poked around for a few moments, closed it, opened another and put Rudy's wallet inside.

'Where do you reckon he hides his stash?'

He looked around. 'Try under the bed – or the wardrobe.'

Under the bed I found some well-used magazines and a crumpled mass of soiled tissues. I yelped and jerked my hand away.

'Ugh!'

'What's up?'

'I think I just found his porn collection.'

I wiped my gloved hand on my jeans, got up and opened the wardrobe. There were a couple of shirts on hangers and a jumble of other clothes piled onto the shelves but I was more interested in the black briefcase at the back of the wardrobe.

'Does that look like it?'

'Could be.'

I cleared a space and laid the case on the floor; as I lifted the lid the rich herbal smell of hash was unmistakable. The case was tightly packed: there were two nine-ounce bars of resin wrapped in red cellophane and a smaller lump of perhaps an ounce. I pressed a thumbnail into one and it was sticky and soft: good quality and not the usual slate-grey, henna-cut stuff. A large ziplock bag held several sheets of blotting paper; each one was printed with dozens of facsimiles of Mickey Mouse's smiling face. A smaller bag bulged with whitish-yellow powder which I thought was probably speed.

There was something else, too: something big and solid in a blue cloth bag, which I passed to Sullivan.

'What's that?'

He undid it and pulled out a thick wad of banknotes.

'Bloody hell.'

He took out block after block of notes and put them on the floor. About a third of the notes were brand new and with paper wrappers, but the others were used and held together with elastic bands. There was so much cash that it seemed like Monopoly money.

'What the fuck?'

We looked at each other in stunned silence.

'Why would he have so much money – and brand new notes from the bank?'

'So much what?' said Billy from the bedroom door.

I groaned.

'I thought you were in bed,' said Sullivan.

Billy shrugged. 'Couldn't sleep, I heard you in here and thought there was something up.'

I closed the lid of the briefcase but it drew Billy's attention to what was on the floor in front of us.

'What's that?'

'Sit down,' sighed Sullivan. 'It's a long story.'

We explained to Billy about Rudy's visitor, the drugs and the money. He listened with widening eyes.

'I didn't have a clue – he was always going out and that and I never knew when he'd come back, he didn't like me asking. Oh my God. What are you going to do?' he said.

'We should leave it,' said Sullivan. 'Put it back where we found it.'

'Yeah, I agree. If it's been stolen we'd get caught; the serial numbers would give it away.'

'Do you reckon he robbed a bank?' said Billy.

'Maybe,' I said. 'I just want to get out of here and pretend we haven't seen any of this.'

'What if we take the used notes and leave the new ones behind?' said Billy.

'No,' I said. 'They could be stolen too. We should leave it.'

'Whatever.'

Sullivan gave me back the notes; with jittery hands I replaced everything where we found it and put the briefcase back in Rudy's wardrobe. I put our gloves in my jeans pocket.

'I don't want to stay here,' said Billy. 'Can I come back with you?'

He picked up the whisky from the kitchen table and drank straight from the bottle.

'Yeah, that's fine,' said Sullivan. 'Get a bag and we'll be on our way.' Billy ran back up the stairs.

'Are you sure?'

'He can't stay here on his own.'

'I'm not in the mood for company right now.'

'He needs us.'

'I need you...I need a hug.'

I buried my face in his shoulder and Sullivan wrapped his arms around me.

'What are we going to do?' I said.

'I don't know.' Sullivan stroked my hair. 'But it'll be alright, OK?'

Billy clomped down the stairs with a rucksack over his shoulder and I dragged myself away from Sullivan's embrace. I went to the fridge and scooped up the eggs, bread and bacon.

'Put them in your rucksack, no use in wasting it if you're coming to stay with us.'

'Oh yeah.'

I had no idea what he'd packed but there was barely room for the groceries in his bag.

'We need to get our stories straight,' I said as we drove back home. I had to concentrate on something to stop my racing brain; I could feel another wave of panic rising and my mouth was as dry as cotton.

'Why?' said Billy from the back seat.

'Because sooner or later someone's going to realise Rudy is missing and the police are going to ask us questions,' I said. 'And we need to be ready; people will have seen us together.'

'So Rudy came out with us last night to the pub,' I continued.

'And afterwards he watched telly with us until we went to bed,' said Sullivan.

'OK.'

'What did we watch?'

'The Young Ones,' said Sullivan and Billy in unison.

I felt sick and started to sweat. 'And Sullivan and I woke up early and went shopping.'

'And Julia very kindly drove Tina home, because you had the flu,' said Sullivan.

'The police don't need to know about me and Tina, do they?'

'We don't want to hide anything, but yeah, good point. Only if they ask,' I said.

'And then this bloke came looking for Rudy, but I said he was out.'

'So you sent him away. He didn't say why he'd come round?'

'No, nothing,' replied Sullivan. 'I thought he was a mate.'

'And you were in bed all the time,' I said.

'Because I had the flu?'

'Yes. And that's why you're staying with us. We couldn't leave you in that place on your own, it's miles from anywhere.'

'Especially not whilst Rudy was out, I didn't know when he'd be back.'

'Exactly.'

'Maybe I should have left him a note or something,' said Billy. 'Let him know where I'd gone.'

I looked at him in the rear view mirror but I couldn't tell whether or not he was serious.

I felt an overwhelming sense of relief when I walked through the front door. I was shaking with exhaustion and hurt all over.

Whilst Sullivan cooked a fry-up I took a hot shower and finally felt nearly clean. I caught sight of myself in the mirror and was shocked to see how pale and pinched I looked, with the same dark blue shadows under my eyes as the others.

The smell of breakfast made my stomach churn.

'I'm going to bed,' I said. 'I'm shattered.'

I took two paracetamol and crawled under the duvet like a wounded animal.

I woke up a couple of hours later and stumbled into the living room – still feeling spacey and still drained in spite of the nap – and saw Billy sitting cross-legged on the living room floor, surrounded by piles of banknotes.

'Billy? What the fuck are you doing?'

He jumped. 'I thought you were asleep.'

'What are you doing? Where's Sullivan?'

Billy shrugged. 'He went out for a walk, said he needed to think.'

'What are you doing?'

'It's alright; I only took the used notes, not the new ones from the bank. There's fifteen thousand and eight hundred pounds here.'

I collapsed on the sofa. 'Oh, Jesus. We can't take it – it's too big a risk. What if Rudy stole that money?'

He looked at me with a glimmer of defiance. 'Sullivan didn't think so.'

'He knows you took this?'

'Yeah, he got a bit cross with me but he said that since I've got it we might as well use it now. Then he went out for a walk.'

'Billy, that briefcase will be covered in your fingerprints. How will you explain that?'

'But I thought of that. I put my gloves on – won't that be alright?'

'I don't know. What else have you taken?'

'Nothing.'

'Nothing? Not even a single trip or an eighth or anything?'

He pursed his lips together and shook his head.

'Are you sure?'

'Yes.'

'OK, I believe you.'

Billy pushed the stacks of banknotes to one side. 'Sullivan said you'd be angry.'

I rubbed my face; I could feel a headache starting to throb behind my eyes. 'Yeah, well. Look, we need to decide what we're going to do next, OK? You can stay here tonight and then on Monday you go back to Baildon, go to uni, and see Tina and act like nothing's the matter. Do you know any of Rudy's friends?'

'No, not really, people come round most days but no.'

'Right. Give it a few days, maybe a week, and then you need to report him missing. Remember what we agreed – that you think he went out early on Sunday morning and you've not seen him since then.'

'What, to the police? I can't go to the police.'

'No, we'll come with you to the uni welfare office and we'll tell them.'

'You'll come with me? Do you promise?'

'Yes. It's in all our best interests to stick together, OK?'

'Suppose so.'

He packed the banknotes back into his rucksack and wouldn't look me in the eye.

Chapter Eight

October 1993

An hour later Sullivan came home, smelling of vodka.

'Did you know about this?'

'Yeah, it'll be fine.'

'*Fine?* There's fifteen grand of stolen money there.'

'Relax, alright?'

'Where have you been?'

'Out.'

'I guessed that. Where "out"?'

'Just out. I needed a walk.' He turned his back on me and sat on the floor next to Billy.

'We can't keep it, there's no telling where Rudy got it from…it's not ours to take. Billy, you've got to put it back.'

'You won't want yours then?' said Sullivan.

I did the maths in my head. Five grand would easily take care of my overdraft, the red gas bill, this month's rent. I sighed.

'We can't. It belongs to Rudy.'

'Fine.'

'No – wait – oh go on, count me in.'

I tried to think of it as compensation for what Rudy had done. I rolled the notes up in an elastic band and hid them in a pair of old boots at the back of the wardrobe. The money made me feel dirty; I didn't want it anywhere I could see it.

By the middle of the afternoon I felt like a caged tiger. Billy and Sullivan were watching a film as if nothing had happened; Sullivan rolled a joint which he and Billy smoked in comfortable silence. I refused it; I couldn't settle and needed to get out of the flat before I suffocated. How could they not feel the same way?

'I'm going for a drive,' I said to no-one in particular.

'Yeah, alright,' said Sullivan without looking up from the TV.

I felt like screaming at them both but instead I drove the Wreck all the way up to Skipton and sat alone, staring into space and watching the sun set in a blaze of orange over the Dales. All I could think about was Rudy, dead and dumped in the mine like rubbish. He didn't deserve to die, I'd overreacted: I should have got dressed – pulled on some jeans first, or I ought to have screamed for Sullivan or Billy instead of lashing out. I couldn't catch hold of all of the slippery thoughts that were wriggling around my brain.

That night we were lying in bed and although the lights were off I was wide awake.

'I'm scared,' I said.

'Why?'

'I can't keep on like this, pretending everything's OK.'

'Like what? We dealt with it.'

'Rudy tried to rape me, for God's sake! I killed him, and you helped me hide his body; we'll both go to prison. Someone will find him and they'll know it was us.'

'It'll be alright. If anyone asks, we don't know where he went.'

I sat up and turned over the pillow. 'Do you think Billy's going to be OK?'

'Yeah, he'll be fine. I'll talk to him tomorrow.'

'What about what we did to Rudy?'

'We sorted it, it'll be alright. Now go to sleep, I'm tired.'

'But he'll have a family and friends! They'll report him missing and then the police will turn up on the doorstep and ask all sorts of questions and I don't think Billy would cope. What if he tells them the truth?'

'I'll talk to him, OK? Like I said, don't worry about it.'

When I finally slept I dreamt of being buried alive: clawing with bloodied fingers at a heavy coffin lid underneath six feet of black earth.

In the morning I felt worse than ever – nauseous and dizzy on top of everything else – and I phoned Gary and told him I'd got the flu.

'There's a lot of it going round,' I said. 'I'll be better in a couple of days.'

I went back to bed but Sullivan was already getting dressed.

'Do you have to get up?'

'Yes.'

'Please, don't go. I'm not well, I need you here.'

'I'll be late for work,' he said and slammed the door on his way out.

I tried to go back to sleep but there was a metallic taste in my mouth as if I was going to throw up, and every time I closed my eyes I had flashbacks of Rudy's hands over my mouth. I pulled the duvet over my face but after another half an hour of lying in bed I couldn't stand it any more.

I put the kettle on but the milk was off; the smell of it made me gag over the sink. I held my breath and poured it away.

'I need to go shopping,' I said to Billy. 'Do you want a lift into town?'

'Do I have to? Can't I stay here a bit longer?'

'You need to go back to uni, like we agreed. Have you got lectures today?

'Yeah, this afternoon.'

'OK, I'll give you a lift back home. Remember what we said?'

'Yeah.'

'Great.'

'Can I leave my money here though?'

'Go on.'

'Thanks,' he grinned. 'You're alright.'

Driving back to Baildon felt surreal. Panic bubbled in my stomach and my palms were so slick with sweat that my hand slipped off the gearstick. At the farmhouse, Billy went to open the door of the Wreck.

'Before you go, I need to ask you something.'

He took his hand off the door handle and looked me with wide eyes. 'Am I in trouble?'

'Oh Billy, no you're not in trouble. But you have to promise me something, alright?

He swallowed and nodded. 'OK.'

'You can't tell anyone what happened; you do know that, don't you?'

'Rudy went out and he's not come back. That's what happened, wasn't it?'

'That's right.'

'But what if he does come back?' he said.

'He won't – he can't.'

He nodded. 'Yeah, OK. Umm...do you want to come in?'

'Thanks, but I can't, sorry. There are some things I've got to do in town.'

I didn't want to admit to Billy that I was too frightened to set foot inside the house.

I felt a bit better during the afternoon: whatever bug I'd picked up seemed to be passing. For minutes at a time I'd forget about Rudy but then reality would hit me again and my imagination turned every car driving along the cobbled street and every footstep outside into the police.

I wondered where Sullivan was. He normally came home just before six if he was working, but there was no sign of him. It was unlike him to be late and not call me first.

He finally walked through the door three hours late, windswept and with beer on his breath.

'Where have you been?'

'Down the pub with Simon and Annette.' He hiccupped and pronounced the words with exaggerated care.

'What, since nine o'clock this morning?

'Give it a rest, will you?'

'We need to talk.'

He sat down on the sofa and sighed. 'What?'

'What are we going to do with the money? How about opening an account at the building society and...'

'No. Can't risk that. Keep it as cash and only spend a tenner at a time, be careful.'

'A tenner? But there's five grand there – let alone what you and Billy have got! It'll take forever to spend it. What about the bills and the rent?'

'I'm going to bed.'

In the morning I woke up to the sound of Sullivan moving about and getting dressed. I squinted at the clock; it was ten past seven.

'Where are you going?'

Sullivan sat on the end of the bed with his back to me and began to lace his boots.

'Work.'

'But you don't work on Tuesdays?'

'They asked me to cover an early delivery.'

I knew he was lying but couldn't be bothered to argue. I slumped back against the pillows and he went out without kissing me goodbye.

I phoned in sick again and went back to bed, but the room started to spin and all I could see in my mind's eye was Rudy lying dead on the flagstoned kitchen floor. As much as I wanted to sleep all day I couldn't, so I got up and went to the kitchen to make some breakfast.

There were piles of dirty cups and plates on the worktop but I shrank back from the sink: the thought of facing the kitchen window with my back to the door was enough to convince me that someone was standing behind me and about to put their hands around my throat. And if I ran the taps I wouldn't hear them over the sound of the water. Maybe I'd get us a takeaway Chinese tonight, and do the dishes afterwards when Sullivan got home. If he came home.

But Rudy's dead, I told myself. *No-one's going to hurt you.* I checked that the door was locked, and filled the sink with hot water and suds. I managed to somehow only look over my shoulder twice in the ten minutes it took me to deal with the dirty crockery but by the end my back was damp with sweat. I lay on the sofa afterwards, feeble with exhaustion.

The Big Issue, 25-31 October 1995
Please Help Us Find Rudolph (Rudy) Baxter (Bradford, West Yorkshire)

Rudy went missing from Baildon, near Bradford, West Yorkshire two years ago on 24th October 1993. He was 20 years old at the time of his disappearance and was studying at Bradford University. His family are concerned for his welfare.

Rudy has contacts in London and the Bradford area. Rudy is urged to contact The Big Issue or the National Missing Person's Helpline for advice and support.

Chapter Nine

October 1993

At lunchtime the phone rang. I dragged myself off the sofa to answer it, hoping it would be Sullivan calling to apologise.

'I saw him!' shouted Billy over phone-box pips. 'I saw Rudy!'

'Oh, hi, it's you.'

'It was Rudy!'

'But you can't have done! He can't be…'

'But I saw him! Near the Uni! It was him, really it was!'

The room started to spin and I sat on the floor, feeling faint. 'Billy, it was probably someone who looked a little bit like him, your mind was playing tricks. I promise you, it can't be.'

'Put my brother on, *he'll* believe me.'

'Sullivan's not here, I'll get him to give you a call later, yeah?'

'No! I'm coming to stay with you again. Rudy'll come back to the house and…'

And find that we've stolen his money, said a voice in my head. But I knew Billy must have made a mistake, we'd put Rudy's body down the mineshaft and he was dead: Sullivan had checked that he wasn't breathing and he had no pulse. Hadn't he? I took a deep breath and the swirling room slowed down a fraction.

'Look, if you want to come back and stay for a few days, that's fine. But I promise you that it wasn't Rudy – you know, it happens sometimes, you think you've seen somebody, but it's not really them.'

'I'm gonna pack now and I'll be there by dinner time. It was him, it really was, and he's gonna kill me.'

Billy arrived on his bike, carrying a rucksack jammed with clothes; a shirt sleeve trailed from the half-closed zip. He looked so pale and haunted that his freckles stood out like a rash. I put the kettle on; it was the only useful thing I could think to do.

'It was in town,' said Billy as he followed me into the kitchen. 'Rudy got off the bus and walked right past me. The weird thing was he didn't have his glasses on but it was definitely him.'

The hairs on my arms stood up: we'd buried Rudy without his glasses.

'How did he look? Was he hurt? Limping, maybe?'

'Dunno.'

'Did he see you?'

'Don't think so.'

Billy sat on our tatty sofa and rolled a joint. He huddled like a refugee under the old tartan blanket that we used as a throw, and all he did was smoke, stare into space and sometimes scratch aimlessly at a spot on his arm. We both only picked at the vegetable curry that I cooked for dinner.

'Are you alright?' I said to Billy once we'd finished pretending to eat.

He'd withdrawn under the blanket again and he was lying on his side, staring into space. A muscle twitched under his left eye and he looked exhausted.

'Fine,' he said in a very small voice.

'Don't you want any dinner?'

'I'm scared.'

'Why?' I sat on the floor next to him but he was lost in his own thoughts. 'Why are you scared? Do you think Rudy's going to come back?'

He didn't say anything.

'Billy, Rudy's not going to hurt you, and you're not in any trouble, I promise. You don't need to be afraid, we'll look after you.'

I wondered if Billy was genuinely ill with the flu: he certainly wasn't himself. I didn't know what else to do or say and the atmosphere in the flat was stifling, so I put the television on. After a couple of hours of channel surfing – flicking from *EastEnders* to the news, to *Red Dwarf* – I went to bed at half past ten.

I couldn't sleep again and stared at the ceiling in the dark, wondering how Sullivan could be out having fun like nothing had happened; thinking about Billy and his utter conviction that he'd seen Rudy.

Sullivan finally came home just after midnight. I heard him fumbling at the front door, trying to get his key in the lock and swearing under his breath. He came straight to bed – stumbling into the chest of drawers on his way – and when he got under the covers I spooned next to him but he pushed me away. Wide awake, I listened to him snore like thunder for the rest of the night.

The next morning I went back to work: I still felt ill and drained but I couldn't face another day cooped up in the flat with Billy.

'Are you feeling better, love?' asked Gary as I stumbled through the door, half an hour late.

'Yeah, thanks.'

He looked me up and down. 'Are you sure you're alright? You'll scare the customers away, looking like that.'

My head felt like it was filled with clay and I jumped every time a customer came through the door. By lunchtime I was shattered from the effort of keeping myself together, so I spent the afternoon in the sanctuary of the back room, cleaning equipment that didn't need cleaning and organising sheets of flash that didn't need re-filing. Somehow I dragged myself through the rest of the day until closing time when I escaped to the relative safety of the flat.

It was dark when I got home and the flat reeked of weed. I flicked on the light to reveal Billy cowering under the blanket on the sofa and still wearing yesterday's clothes. The ashtray was heaped with roach-ends.

'What's the matter?'

He turned to look at me, his eyes as round and dark as cigarette burns. 'Rudy's come back and he's going to kill me because of what you did to him...and he'll tell the police what really happened, and we'll all end up in prison.'

'Rudy won't go to the police, he's dead.'

'But I saw him! You lied to me, he isn't dead is he, you're making it up. Why are you both lying?'

'Oh, Billy.'

'H...he'll say the gear's mine,' he said. 'After all, we've got the money, haven't we? I thought...I thought that I was helping you by taking it, all I wanted was to make everything better...'

'Rudy's dead, Billy. And nobody is going to prison, alright?'

'Do you swear?' He looked at me with those cratered eyes.

'Yes, I swear,' I said and hugged him. The blanket draped over his shoulder fell off to reveal an ugly, bleeding sore where he'd picked and scratched at his arm; his white T-shirt was covered in dried blood.

'Jesus. Here, let me take a look at that.'

'No.' Billy pulled his arm away.

'Come on; let me clean it up for you. It'll get infected.'

I reached out to take his hand and he curled up into a ball under the blanket. I got a basin of warm water and antiseptic and cleaned him up as best I could, but all the while Billy stared silently at the wall.

Sullivan was still out when I got up the next morning, but he never stayed out all night without letting me know where he was. I felt panic rise in my stomach and I couldn't help but think of him in a police cell somewhere.

I made Billy some tea before I left for work – he barely mumbled an acknowledgement – and I spent the day watching the door hoping that Sullivan would show up and apologise for not coming home. I got desperate enough to phone the flat from the office twice during the day when Gary was busy with customers, but there was no answer.

The moment we closed I dashed home, my stomach in knots and with a feeling that something terrible had happened. Once again the flat was silent and dark and Billy was lying on the sofa.

'Hi,' I said to his motionless form. 'Any sign of Sullivan?'

He made a grunt that I took to mean no and I felt my heart sink. I called Simon; he was the only person I could think of who might know where Sullivan might be – but there was no reply there either.

He finally came home as I was making dinner and debating whether I should only have cooked for two.

'Where have you been?'

'Down the pub.'

'Where were you last night?'

'I had too much to drink and Simon let me sleep on the sofa.'

I slammed spaghetti onto plates. 'I don't believe you. What's going on?'

'Nothing's going on. I went out with Simon and got too pissed to come home so I crashed at their place, that's all.'

'So if I phone Annette she'll tell me the same?'

'Do what you like,' he said. 'Hurry up, I'm ravenous.'

It was all I could do not to throw the spaghetti bolognaise in his face. He ate dinner like a starving man and went out again as soon as he'd finished, leaving Billy and me to another lonely evening watching TV.

Chapter Ten

October 1993

The next day was Friday and my day off. I woke up alone at half past seven and lay in bed, thinking that it was high time we reported Rudy missing. After fretting for an hour I got up and roused Billy with a mug of tea.

'Wake up; we're going to the welfare office.'

He groaned and turned over.

'Come on, you know what we agreed, we've got to do it.'

'No.'

'We'll be fine; we talked about this the other day, OK?'

He rubbed his face and dragged himself off the sofa; for a moment I thought about waiting for Sullivan to come back, but I pushed the idea away. We could cope on our own.

'Aren't you going to have a shower?' Billy had a musky, animal smell and was still wearing the three-day-old top that was stiff with dried blood down one arm.

He shook his head. 'Don't want to.'

I went to his rucksack and pulled out a shirt. 'You can't go out like that. Get changed, at least.'

I helped him put on the clean shirt but he fumbled so badly I had to do the buttons up for him. His face was red and flushed and when I put my hand on his forehead he felt feverishly hot.

The drive across town was painfully slow in the morning rush hour and as we crawled up to the third set of red traffic lights I wondered whether I was doing the right thing.

'So, what are we going to tell them?'

Billy squirmed in his seat and chewed his thumbnail.

'Billy?'

He stared out of the window and didn't reply.

'I'll talk to them, shall I?'

The welfare office was in the student union building; it felt as if lifetimes had passed since Sullivan kissed me there on our first date.

The room smelt of instant coffee and a spider plant sagged on top of the fridge. A woman greeted us with a smile and introduced herself as Deepa.

'Oh, um, hi,' I said. Jesus, I was getting as bad as Billy. 'Err; we'd like to report a missing person please. Um – this is Billy Sullivan, he's my boyfriend's brother – he's a student here and...and he's not seen his housemate since Saturday. Rudy, he's called. He's a student as well.'

It took us nearly half an hour. Deepa called her supervisor, and the two of them had a huddled discussion in the corner of the office. Although I overheard snatches of conversation I couldn't make sense of what they were saying. Billy was shaking and I wanted to run away but instead settled for fidgeting and staring out the window. Deepa glanced at me once or twice, which made me feel even more nervous.

Eventually she opened a notebook and took down our details and Rudy's name and address.

'Now what will you do?' I said.

She closed her book. 'We'll contact his parents; Rudy's probably gone home for a few days and not let anyone know. I'm sure there's nothing to worry about.'

'What about the police? Do you want us to give statements or something?'

Her smile vanished. 'Police? Oh, goodness me, no. Why, do you think that something might have happened to him?'

Billy leapt up from his seat, wild-eyed. 'Why's she looking at me like that? Haven't you told her he's not coming back?'

'Hey, shush. It's alright; she's trying to help us,' I said and put my hand on his shoulder, pushing him back into his chair. Deepa froze with her pen still in her hand and she looked at Billy, then me, and back to Billy.

'Sorry about Billy,' I said to her. 'He's ever so upset, he thinks something bad must have happened to Rudy. He doesn't mean it.'

I turned to him. 'Come on love, I'll take you home. Thanks for your help Deepa, will you get in touch if you hear anything?'

'Of course,' she said.

I bundled Billy out of the office and into to the Wreck.

'What was all that about?'

'But it's true,' he said, frowning. 'You promised me.'

'Billy, you mustn't say things like that! You'll get us all into trouble. For God's sake, you need to think first before you blurt things out. What if Deepa does decide to tell the police? What will happen to us all then?'

'I'm sorry.'

'Sorry might not be enough.' My face flushed with raging fury. I felt like shaking him.

'Is there anything else you want to tell me?'

He stared out the windscreen and didn't answer.

'You're a bloody idiot, Billy Sullivan. You wait until I tell your brother what you did.'

I drove back to the flat in furious silence. When we got in Billy went straight to the sofa and climbed under the blanket. Sullivan was still out so I shut myself in the bedroom and tried to read a book. I was still so infuriated with Billy that I couldn't bear to be in the same room as him.

When Sullivan came back at lunchtime I couldn't figure out whether I was relieved to see him or not.

'Where have you been?'

He scratched his chin and looked past me, out of the window. 'Band practice, it ended up being an all-nighter, we were on a roll and didn't finish until seven this morning.'

I wanted to be angry but could only feel a dull sensation of detachment, as if I was on the wrong side of a dirty pane of glass.

'Really?'

'Yeah, really.'

I went to hug him, half-expecting him to push me away but instead he put his arm around me and we stood in the bedroom, with my head buried in his shoulder. I was too numb to feel anything at all.

Mojo

December 1995

The Wages of War – Sydenham Poyntz

Darkly brilliant follow up album with attitude from Bradford indie outfit.

Twenty-something Bradford rockers Sydenham Poyntz's second album is truly something special. Building on the success of 1994's *Honesty, The Wages of War* is jam-packed with tight, nigh-perfect three-minute slices of classic indie rock. Showcasing 1960s-style heavy R&B as well as effortlessly melodic guitar pop, there's not a dud track to be found.

This record contains some of the band's most beautiful songs to date; from the straight up rock of *Patience is No Virtue* and *Blaze* to the idyllic, poignant ballad of *BD1*, a love song to Friday nights in their hometown. This is a band that richly deserves wider recognition.

●●●●●

Chapter Eleven

October 1993

We somehow muddled through the next few days. Billy spent his time lying on the sofa, lost in his own thoughts, smoking weed and barely eating. Sullivan was hardly ever at home and I dreaded waking up in the morning because the stress of not knowing where he was made me feel constantly dizzy and sick.

I was working late on the Thursday, cleaning up and washing the floor because I couldn't bear another evening in the flat on my own with Billy. It was an inky dark, rainy night and the street lamps reflected sulphurous pools of light on the pavement outside.

There was a crash as someone pushed the door open and I jumped – for a terrible second I thought Rudy had come back after all, but it was Sullivan. He was soaking; water streamed in torrents off his leather jacket and hair.

'Oh. Hi.'

'It's Billy. He's been arrested.'

'What, for Rudy...?'

'No.'

He paced up and down, leaving black boot-marks on the clean lino, and told me what had happened when he'd got home at lunchtime after another all-night rehearsal. He'd found Billy on the sofa, staring at the ceiling and wrapped in the blanket. He explained how Billy first of all stayed silent when Sullivan asked him how he was and when he was going back to uni, but then Billy told him about Rudy's ghost that he'd seen in the flat, and how Rudy was blaming Billy for what we had done to him.

In desperation I asked if he was joking, but he shook his head and said Billy had shouted something that didn't make sense and then run out of the flat; Sullivan had followed but couldn't keep up. He'd given up searching the streets after an hour, and had no idea where his brother had gone until the police phoned, on account of Sullivan being named as next of kin on Billy's organ donor card. They told him they'd had to section Billy and send him to the mental hospital in Menston after finding him half-naked and screaming on top of the War Memorial.

'Shit. Does your mum know?'

'Not yet, I've got to phone her.'

I closed up the shop and gave Sullivan a lift home. The flat looked like a bomb had gone off, with Billy's clothes strewn across the front room. I tidied up whilst Sullivan talked to his mum and told her Billy had been taken ill and was in hospital for observation, although he didn't think it was serious.

As I was folding Billy's jeans I found a packet of Rizlas and a big lump of soft and sticky hash in the front pocket. It was wrapped in a piece of red cellophane.

I quickly searched his bag, but couldn't find anything else that he might have taken from Rudy's stash. There was no sign of any money either; I presumed that Sullivan had hidden his and Billy's share, and I didn't want to know where.

Sullivan hung up and sat on the sofa. 'She's coming to visit first thing tomorrow.'

'You didn't tell her which hospital he's in.'

'I didn't want to get her worried. I told her I'd explain it in the morning.'

'Do you think that's a good idea?'

He shrugged.

'What do you want for dinner?'

'Don't bother about cooking, I'm going out.'

'I need to talk to you…I'm really worried about Billy.'

'I'm only going for a couple of pints with Simon, we can talk later.'

'Don't be late...' I said, but he was already out the door.

I hardly slept again that night, thinking about Billy and wondering where Sullivan had gone this time – and who he was with. He still hadn't come home when Barbara arrived early the next morning.

'Hi Barbara, come in.'

She sat on our sofa and looked around the room, red-eyed. 'Where's Jeremy?'

'I'm afraid Sullivan – Jeremy – had to go out. He got a phone call this morning, something about covering an urgent delivery at work. I'm sure he won't be long.'

The disappointed look she gave me said she didn't believe a word. I sat down on the sofa next to her and silently cursed him for deliberately leaving me to break the news.

'OK, you know Billy's in hospital, right?'

She nodded. 'Is everything alright? Jeremy didn't say very much on the phone yesterday.'

'Well, the thing is, the doctors think he's had some sort of nervous breakdown...they've taken him to the psychiatric hospital to do some tests.'

'My Billy's in a *mental hospital*? Oh no, no, he can't be...' She started to cry and dabbed at her eyes with a hanky.

She looked so lost and sad that I reached out and gave her a hug; she was heartbreakingly thin and frail under her anorak.

'Would you like a lift to the hospital?' I said once she'd stopped crying. 'Jeremy can meet us there.'

'Thank you dear, you're very kind.'

Sullivan staggered home as we were leaving. One glance – the puffy eyes, the smell of stale beer – told me that he'd been up all night again.

'I'm taking your mum to see Billy,' I said with brittle politeness that was more for her benefit than his. 'Are you coming?'

Sullivan climbed obediently into the back seat of the Wreck and I drove north over the river. As we passed the turn-off to Baildon I gritted my teeth and put my foot down: the name on the signpost along with the sight of the great wide expanse of moorland made my heart race.

'Are you OK there in the back?' I said.

'Yeah.'

Barbara looked uncomfortable perched in the Wreck's passenger seat and she grabbed her handbag every time the ancient suspension bounced over a pothole.

'When did you last see Billy?' she asked.

'He came round yesterday,' said Sullivan. 'He was a bit quiet.'

'Oh, Jeremy. You were meant to look after him.'

'I know, mum. But our kid was fine, he was settling into college, enjoying himself.'

'Was it drugs? Was Billy taking drugs?'

'No, mum.'

'Then why on Earth has he had this thing – this breakdown?'

'I don't know. Maybe it was stress.'

'I'm sure he's going to be fine,' I said to no-one in particular. I wished I could believe it.

Chapter Twelve

October-November 1993

Billy's ward was in a remote wing of the psychiatric hospital: with the enormous clock tower, the barred windows and echoing parquet floors it was the very picture of an old-fashioned asylum. The sight of the place made me shudder.

A doctor escorted us down a seemingly endless green corridor to a side room off the observation ward, where Billy was lying on a narrow hospital bed and staring into space. He was swamped by a pair of green pyjamas several sizes too large and he was as luminously pale as a Victorian saint. I grabbed Sullivan's hand; he squeezed mine back. He looked terrified.

'Hello, love,' said Barbara but Billy didn't respond.

'Can he hear us?' she asked the doctor.

'Yes,' he said. 'Do talk to him. It can be a great help.'

'What's the matter with him?' I asked.

'The preliminary diagnosis is something called catatonia,' he replied. 'It's a symptom, rather than an illness in itself.'

'Is he going to get better?'

'It's difficult to tell at this stage,' the doctor said. 'It all depends what triggered the episode in the first place.'

'What does that mean?'

'There are a number of different types of medication that can help people in Billy's condition. We hope to see some sort of improvement in the next few days.'

'But what if he doesn't get better? What then?'

'We need to give Billy some time to let the drugs work. We'll let you know if there's any change.'

Afterwards, I drove the three of us back home but it felt like a wake and none of us quite knew what to say.

'How's work, Jeremy? Are you keeping busy?'

'Yeah, it's alright.'

'And Julia, what about you?'

'Yeah, alright, thanks.'

'I always thought tattooing was a funny job for a girl. Have you ever thought of doing something secretarial instead?'

I said nothing and instinctively pulled the left sleeve of my jumper down to my wrist: Gary had done me a purple Celtic knot design on my arm three months previously. I offered Barbara a cup of tea but she declined, saying she had to drive home to Salford before it got dark.

'What do we do now?' I said to Sullivan once she'd left.

'I don't know.' I held his hand and his fingers clung to mine.

'Hey…it'll be OK.'

'Did he say anything to you – was there any sign that this was going to happen?'

'No. Well, he went a bit weird when we were at the welfare office.'

'You what?'

'We went there last week to report Rudy missing. You weren't around. Billy got quite upset, actually.'

'You shouldn't have done that.'

'We had to. You should have been there.'

He shrugged.

I felt a surge of rage: how could he be so casual about something so important?

'Look, the police will want to interview us; they'll get our details from the university.'

'How come?'

'When Billy and I reported Rudy missing they took our contact details down in case they needed to get in touch.'

'And you gave it to them?'

'I had to make it look like we were doing it for real, and it would have seemed weird if someone else had reported it first – anyway, they would have had Billy's address already.'

He sat on the sofa, put his head in his hands and looked for a moment as if he was about to cry. 'Yeah, fair enough.'

'We let Billy down, we both did. I should have seen it coming, the way he was acting...'

'Yeah, I know. When he gets better I'll find a way to make it up to him.'

Over the next couple of weeks I couldn't help but think Sullivan was avoiding me. Every few days he didn't come home of an evening, blaming band practice or uncharacteristically late nights in the pub with Simon: normally we did everything and went everywhere together. If I asked him what was wrong he insisted it was nothing, until eventually I gave up asking.

The cloying, nauseous feeling I'd had on and off since Baildon was still bothering me: I could barely eat anything without wanting to be sick and my clothes began to hang off me. I thought about going to the doctor's, but couldn't face the inevitable prescription for sleeping tablets that would solve nothing.

One particularly lonely evening I tried to block everything out by aimlessly flicking between channels on the TV and smoking joint after joint until I was clammy white and so light-headed I could hardly stand. All it did was make me feel sicker than ever.

'Are you seeing someone else?' I challenged Sullivan when he'd stayed out for the third night in a week.

'Don't be silly.'

'I know, but you've been acting weird, you're always out, I never know where you are or what time you'll be home. I don't know what's going on any more.' I sniffed back tears.

He sat down on the sofa and turned on the television without looking at me. 'We've got a tour booked, OK? We've been busy rehearsing; I didn't want to say anything until it was confirmed.'

'A tour! But that's amazing news! You kept that quiet?'

'Yeah, it's a bit last-minute. Some American group have got a new album out and their support has cancelled. Turns out the promoter's from Leeds, he came to one of our gigs last year. There's ten dates, all paid at union rates.'

'Oh my God, that's brilliant. When is it? What's the band you're supporting?'

‘We leave tomorrow morning. Edinburgh, London, Manchester, all over.’

‘*Tomorrow*?’

‘That’s what I said,’ said Sullivan and went to the bedroom to pack.

Chapter Thirteen

November-December 1993

I was shopping in Morrisons the following weekend when I saw Simon and Annette in the bakery aisle. At first I thought was going mad too, seeing people who weren't there. Simon, Jason, Rob and Sullivan were away on the road, five days down and another seven left to go, not that I was keeping count. I looked again and Annette gave me a tight nod of acknowledgement.

'Oh, hello, I wasn't expecting to see you.'

My brain went into overdrive trying to process what I was seeing; making sure it really was them. Despite the fact that they were Bradford's very own Odd Couple – Simon short, plump and prematurely bald and Annette six feet tall, Swedish and with blonde hair that reached her waist – I didn't trust my eyes any more.

'Aren't you on the tour with the rest of Sydenham Poyntz? Have you got a night off or something?' I felt a surge of stupid hope that Sullivan was planning to surprise me with a visit in between gigs, maybe everything was going to be alright after all...

'Tour?' said Simon. He seemed to struggle with the word.

'You know, the American band – the one with the promoter from Leeds?'

Annette looked at me with a cool stare; her expression was unreadable. 'I think you are mistaken,' she said. 'There is no tour.'

'No tour? But where's Sullivan? He said there were ten dates and you were playing all over the country – I don't understand?'

'He's at our place,' said Simon. He wriggled and stared at the floor: a naughty child caught telling tales on his playmate. 'He said the two of you had a row and that you'd chucked him out – he's staying with us. Didn't you know?'

They told me afterwards that I'd fainted, right there in the supermarket. Annette got the manager to phone for an ambulance but I came round, feeling dizzy and humiliated, before it arrived. They persuaded me to go to hospital for a check up and Annette wanted to come with me but I refused. I insisted I was fine, I'd just forgotten to eat breakfast, but wondering all the while what the hell Simon was going to tell Sullivan. *'Mate, your missus has gone barmy, we saw her in Morrisons and she's told everyone that the band's gone on tour and then she passed out, she's lost it if you ask me...'*

I felt like a fraud during the ambulance ride to the Infirmary but the staff in A&E were brilliant: they gave me the full once over and ran some tests. I stuck to the story about being tired and run down, having the flu and not eating properly, but with hindsight it should have been obvious that I was pregnant.

Ten weeks, the hospital told me after they did a scan, although I was so beside myself with shock that I refused to look at the ultrasound picture, and a well-meaning nurse cooed over the printout until I broke down in tears. I couldn't think of it as a baby; it felt like an alien.

I lay on a hard trolley in a cubicle, wearing scratchy paper knickers and a gaping robe. I tried to work out dates and how it could have happened, when I could have forgotten to take a pill, how I'd managed to be so careless, but everything seemed fragmented. I couldn't pin my thoughts down for more than a second.

I jumped as Sullivan pulled open the curtain.

'Are you alright? Annette told me what happened.'

'Yeah.' The thought of talking to him left me exhausted.

'You look awful. What's the matter?'

'Thanks...I fainted. It's nothing.'

'Look, I'm sorry, alright? Everything – Rudy, Billy – it all got too much, you know? I needed some space to sort my head out.'

I stared at the wall. 'Go home. I'm fine.'

'Can I get you anything?'

'Just go, will you?'

'If you're sure you'll be OK?'

Later that afternoon the hospital discharged me with a letter to take to my GP and a glossy leaflet stressing the importance of healthy eating during pregnancy. I took a taxi back to West Bowling and somehow after our conversation I expected to Sullivan to be there, but there was no sign that he'd come home: no bag of clothes on the bedroom floor, no leather jacket thrown carelessly over the back of the sofa. It took a few minutes for it to sink in that he'd gone back to Simon's instead.

When I realised what he'd done – that he really had left me – it felt as if the ground had been ripped from under my feet. I lay on the sofa and cried myself to sleep.

I got rid of it. I had no choice; I was in no state to look after myself, let alone a child. There was no difficult decision to make, no options to weigh up: I knew there was no way I could go through with having a baby on my own.

I explained all this to a sympathetic doctor when I went to the GP's, feeling twitchy and dry-mouthed. He didn't bat an eyelid when I started crying halfway through the appointment.

I was booked into the hospital for the abortion the following week. Signing the consent forms felt surreal, as if I were watching myself over my own shoulder. My pen hovered over the Next of Kin box but in the end I left it blank. Nobody knew I was there.

Not long after I came round from the anaesthetic I dozed off again and had a dream that Sullivan had somehow discovered where I was and cried when he found out what I'd done; it turned out he'd desperately wanted children after all.

I lay on my side waiting for the cramps to pass and tried to find some trace of emotion about what I'd done, but the only thing I felt was a tiny glimmer of relief.

I took two days off work and told Gary I'd had food poisoning.

On my first day back I felt hollow and fuzzy-headed. I drew the first client's design on the wrong shoulder and when he pointed out my mistake I burst into tears and ran into the back room.

'Time of the month is it, love?' said Gary. 'Best sit down and have a cuppa, eh?'

'I'm fine,' I said. 'I just need some fresh air...'

I went to the corner shop for some baccy and a can of Coke. There was a queue: a kid in front didn't have enough change for his pasty and was arguing with the shopkeeper. I tuned out and flicked through a copy of the *Telegraph & Argus* that was lying on the counter.

The headline at the bottom of the front page jumped out. There was a photo of Rudy and the sight of him made my battered insides churn. I bought the paper and forced myself to read the rest of the article in spite of the nausea rising in my throat.

Bradford Telegraph & Argus

3 December 1993

Police Appeal For Missing Student

West Yorkshire Police are urgently appealing for information on the whereabouts of missing Rudy Baxter (20), a second year Engineering student at Bradford University.

Rudy, originally from Palmers Green, London, was last seen over a month ago in Baildon and his worried family say his disappearance is out of character.

"Rudy is a loving son and brother, and we appeal for him to come home," his mother told the *Telegraph & Argus*. "Rudy, if you're in

> any sort of trouble, we won't be angry, we only need to know that you're safe."
>
> Mr Baxter is described as white with short light brown hair, 5'11" and medium to heavy build. He was wearing jeans and a grey parka style coat when he was last seen.
>
> Please contact Bradford police station on 0274 376600 with any information.

I bought a paper and could hardly concentrate for the rest of the afternoon, thinking about what I'd read. If the police were involved, surely they would want to talk to us? I had to let Sullivan know: assuming the police hadn't already visited him.

After work I drove straight round to Simon's with the newspaper on the passenger seat. A glimmer of light shone from a gap in the red velvet curtains in the front window; I leant on the bell and counted to thirty before Sullivan eventually answered. He looked like a stranger: he was tired and puffy with unwashed hair and a week's worth of beard. His big toe poked through a hole in his sock.

He sniffed. 'Oh, it's you.'

I brandished the newspaper. 'Have you seen this?'

'What?'

'We need to talk. Can I come in?'

'Now's not a good time.'

'It's important.'

I pushed past him and went into the front room. There was a woman there who I didn't know, wearing a purple tie-dyed skirt and what I recognised as Sullivan's favourite jumper. She looked at me with glittering, amused eyes and tucked a gerbil-coloured dreadlock behind her ear. A smeared mirror lay on the coffee table, half-hidden by a magazine. It was scattered with crumbs of powder; a razor blade and a rolled-up ten-pound note lay on top. I pretended I hadn't seen it.

'Oh. I'm sorry, I didn't realise...'

'I'm Siobhan,' she said. 'You must be Julia.' She stretched luxuriously and stood up.

'I'll see you in the pub later, babe,' she said to Sullivan.

'Yeah, see you later.' She kissed him on the cheek, put on her overcoat and left.

The room suddenly felt too hot. 'Who's she?'

'Siobhan? No-one, she's just a friend.'

'Liar.' I made a face and pushed the paper into his hands. 'Read the front page. It's about Rudy.'

'So what?' he said as he scanned the headline. 'We know he's missing.'

'But it's official now, it's taken this long for someone to take it seriously. I bet they've found the drugs and the rest of the money as well...'

'Whatever.'

'Is there any more news about Billy?'

'No.'

'Have you been to see him?'

'He doesn't recognise me.'

'But he's your brother! You can't abandon him in that place! It's your fault; you left us to manage on our own.'

'My fault? How is any of this my fault?'

'We should have called an ambulance, explained that it was an accident – you told me to get rid of him, and you helped so you're a part of all this as much as me. If it wasn't for your sodding criminal record we could've dealt with it properly. You've seen this; now the police will get our details from the university. I didn't think...'

'You said it.'

'What?'

'You didn't think. That's always been your problem, you never think about anyone except yourself.'

'Oh, for God's sake.'

'What?'

'What about us?' My voice broke and I swallowed tears.

'You made it clear at the hospital you didn't want me around. You can't come here now, changing your mind. It's too late.'

'But I was ill, I wasn't thinking straight!'

'How can you expect me to live with what you did – and with what's happened to Billy because of it? He's only in that state because of you.'

'Oh, fuck off. When are you going to collect the rest of your stuff?'

'I'll get Simon to come round with the van.'

'Good. Don't forget to leave your key.'

I snatched the paper back from Sullivan and walked out, but barely made it back to the Wreck before the tears came.

Melody Maker

10 February 1996

Sydenham Poyntz Munich Show Ends in Chaos

With the release of their second album, *The Wages of War,* Bradford's favourite indie rockers Sydenham Poyntz appeared to have it all. With the album in the Top 10 and a fifteen-date European tour scheduled, you could be forgiven for thinking that the band had the world at their feet.

But loyal fans were left shocked when front man Sullivan cancelled the remainder of the tour after a shambolic set in Munich last Thursday night.

Gig-goers reported that bassist Simon Gray began playing erratically during the opening number, throwing his instrument into the audience and leaving the stage. Gray was reported to have been hospitalised with exhaustion following his early exit from the set.

"Unfortunately Simon was taken unwell during the Munich show," Sullivan told

Melody Maker. "The doctors think he has a virus so it's very important that he takes it easy for a few weeks.

"I'd like to apologise to all our fans and we hope to reschedule the cancelled shows later in the year." The rest of the band was unavailable for comment.

But Sydenham Poyntz fans were not placated by the band's statement. "We paid DM40 for our tickets," said a man who gave his name as Andreas. "And now they tell us that there are no refunds. We have been treated very poorly."

A twenty-three year old man was reported to have been slightly injured in the incident.

Gigs in Paris, London and Stockholm have been postponed indefinitely.

Chapter Fourteen

December 1993

I went to visit Billy on a snowy afternoon a fortnight before Christmas.

'Hi, how are you?' He said nothing and looked through me with lifeless eyes.

'Are they looking after you alright? How's the food?'

He didn't reply.

'Ummm...work's OK, we're pretty busy at the minute, and I've been doing a lot of overtime. It's good – I mean I don't need the money, do I, but now that Sullivan's staying with Simon and Annette – I guess he's told you all about that, hasn't he – it's nice to have something to take my mind off things, you know?

He started to weep and tears ran silently down his cheeks.

'Oh God, I'm so sorry, I didn't mean to upset you.'

I offered him a tissue but he didn't move and stayed crying silently, staring at something invisible a thousand yards away.

'Look, I'm sorry, I'd best be going. I'll come back again another time when you're feeling better, eh?'

On my way out I asked a nurse – a tall man with the grey flowing locks and beard of a middle-aged Jesus – whether Billy had any chance of recovery.

'There's always hope,' he replied.

That evening I watched the nine o'clock news where Rudy's family appealed at a press conference for information on his whereabouts. His brother Martin did most of the talking: his parents were stunned into mute terror by the questions and paparazzi flashbulbs and they could only mumble a plea for Rudy to come home. Part of me wanted to make the anonymous call to let them know where he was buried, but I couldn't do it. I turned the television off as his father began to stammer a few more words to the waiting cameras.

My need to protect myself – and Sullivan, even now – outweighed my need to help Rudy's family. I hated how selfish I'd become; it made me feel mean and dirty.

Sullivan had left a bottle of vodka in the freezer when he left. I poured three inches of the syrupy liquid into a glass and drank myself to sleep.

'Sorry I'm late,' I said to Gary as I stumbled into work, feeling miserable and hungover.

'Thought you'd gone off sick again.'

'Yeah, sorry – I slept through the alarm. Don't worry; I'll make the time up.'

'Good. Someone came in first thing, asking for you.'

'Who? Was it Sullivan?' A swell of hope flared up but faded as quickly as it came.

'No.' He looked confused. 'Another bloke – a big guy with a shaved head and a gold tooth. Didn't like the look of him.'

I shook my head, Gary's description didn't sound like anyone I knew.

'Said he was looking for Ruby, said you might know where he was.'

'He? *Ruby*? Oh...'

'Anyway, I told him you'd be in later, he didn't look too happy if you ask me. Who's Ruby?'

'I don't know.'

I fled to the back room and was shaking so much I could hardly take off my coat. Who the hell was looking for Rudy – was he the police, or was he Rudy's dealer, missing his money? More to the point, how did he know where to find me?

I spent the rest of the day waiting for the guy to come back, and only felt a whisper of relief when I got back home that evening.

The next day was Gary's day off and I didn't want to go into work on my own. I still felt worn out from the previous day, and wondered whether the guy looking for Rudy would turn up again. I changed my mind three times about going into the studio before I even got out of bed.

In the end common sense won and I crawled out from under the duvet at nine o'clock. I couldn't justify a sick day because we had a customer booked in: Malcolm, a regular client who was scheduled for the final touches to complete his flaming-skeleton-on-a-Harley back piece that'd I'd been working on for a couple of months. He had told me at the first session that it was a fortieth birthday present from his wife and privately I thought the design was hideous, but I bit my tongue and politely listened to his biker-gang war stories whilst inking his immense and freckled back.

Hardly anyone wanted a tattoo just before Christmas and he was our only booked customer. I figured I could get the final bits of shading on the flames finished by mid-afternoon and then close up before it got dark. I was certain nobody would dare try to make trouble in front of Malcolm: he was built like an ox and had a golden beard that reached down to his belt. Except that he called first thing to rebook because his daughter had picked up a bug from school and he had to look after her. I was on my own after all.

The thought of being alone in the shop left me terrified: every few minutes I looked out of the window to make sure there was no-one about to come in, but there was nothing to see except a few people trudging through the slush on the pavement outside. I flicked the bolt on the front door but one of the screws had been loose for weeks and it was obvious the lock wouldn't have withstood anyone who had the slightest inclination to get in.

To take my mind off things I cleaned everything I could find. I unscrewed the light fittings and wiped the dust out with a damp cloth, I found one of Gary's old copies of *The Sun* in the bin out the back and used it to clean the windows and I even scrubbed out the filthy and freezing outside toilet that hadn't seen a drop of bleach all year. My thin latex gloves were no protection against the bitter weather and when I finished my hands were red and chapped with cold.

By lunchtime I had tidied and cleaned everything I could. I was fed up and was half-tempted to close up early but dared not in case Gary found out. I wondered if I could make up some domestic emergency that meant I'd had to go home, but lying about a burst pipe was tempting fate in the middle of winter with snow on the ground and more forecast. I told myself that sitting in the flat alone wasn't something to look forward to either, so I made a cup of tea, ate a pot noodle and flicked through a back issue of *Classic Car* to pass the time.

The more I tried to push Rudy, Billy and Sullivan out of my mind the more I wondered what Sullivan was doing. Was he rehearsing with the band – or was he with Siobhan somewhere? The thought of the two of them together made me feel queasy; as if I'd eaten a whole box of chocolates in one go.

I wasn't surprised when the stranger turned up and knocked on the bolted door an hour before closing. Even before he opened his mouth and revealed the gold crown I knew he was the same man who had spoken to Gary. My hands started to shake.

'Hi. Come in. Can I help?'

'Maybe,' he said. He was smoking a cigarette that he held cupped in one hand.

'I'm sorry but you can't smoke that in here.'

'Yes I can.'

He tapped ash on the floor and turned to look at the pages of flash nearest the door.

'A...are you looking for something in particular?'

'*Someone* in particular.' He dropped the cigarette butt on the lino and ground it out with his heel. I winced.

'Do you mean Gary? He's not here, but if you want to leave a message...' I could have kicked myself; I'd as good as told him that I was on my own.

'I'm looking for Rudy. I think you know where he is.' The gold tooth flashed at me again.

'I don't know.'

'How's Billy? I heard he wasn't very well.'

'No, he's not...'

He kept looking at the designs, not making eye contact with me. 'A little bird told me he took something he shouldn't have. Some things that weren't his.'

All I could hear was the rush of blood in my ears.

'I think I'll have that one.'

He fingered a small triangular Celtic design. I felt frozen and didn't know what to do: I didn't think he really wanted a tattoo, but I had no choice about maintaining the charade that he was only another customer. If only Gary was here...

The man watched me squirm as I removed the sheet and asked about colours; he told me he wanted it in green.

'Great, that'll be forty pounds. We only take cash and if you need to go to the bank first there's a cash dispenser down on Leeds Road.'

'No.'

'Oh, OK. Where would you like the design? A lot of people like to have that on the upper arm...' I gestured weakly at my own shoulder.

I was horrified when he sat on the couch, unbuckled his jeans and let them puddle around his ankles. He had some other tattoos – a swirly black tribal marking on one calf and something that looked like a badly executed skull and roses design poking out from his waistband.

He grinned evilly and pointed at his groin. I could hardly bear to look.

'Right here.'

'Are you sure? That's a very…um…sensitive area…'

'Yeah, I'm sure. You got a problem with that?'

'No…it's fine. If you're certain…?'

The man lay down on the couch with his hands behind his head. He watched me hesitate as I picked up the disposable razor and alcohol scrub.

'What's the matter? Are you nervous?'

I grimaced; my face was inches from his crotch as I bent over to start prepping.

'I'm going to have to shave the area first, is that OK? It helps stop the risk of infection.'

I looked at him for some sign of acknowledgment but he shrugged and looked at the ceiling, his arms folded behind his head.

With shaky hands I gloved up and shaved the hair from the top of his thigh, barely an inch from the edge of his blue Calvin Kleins. I tried to empty my mind of everything apart from the tattoo whilst I cleaned the area with alcohol gel.

'OK, this might sting slightly. It's to sterilise the area before I start.' I looked up and saw he was grinning.

'And now I'm going to draw on the design. You're still sure you want to go ahead with this?'

'Stop chattering and get on with it.'

I traced the outline on and expected all the while for him to change his mind or to say something: as a rule clients talked a fair amount from nerves, but he was mocking me with his silence.

I squeezed the ink into tubes and fitted a three-needle for the outline.

'OK, you'll feel a bit of discomfort to begin with, but take a few slow, deep breaths and the pain will ease up, but if you need me to stop for a minute or two you only have to ask, it's absolutely fine. Are you ready?'

'I told you to get on with it.'

I started up the machine, willed my hands to stay steady and began tracing the border.

'You know where Rudy is.'

I stopped what I was doing. 'Who?'

'Don't give me that. Carry on.'

I did as I was told, and tried my best to focus on the design. 'No, I don't.'

'People are worried about him.'

'I'm sorry to hear that, but I can't help.'

'The thing is, your idiot mate knows something that might help me. Except he's not talking much, is he?'

'Who are you?'

The man laughed. 'You ask a lot of questions.'

'I…'

'Now hurry up. Jesus, what's the matter with you?'

I said nothing and fixed my attention on the tattoo. I looked up once, when I changed the needles over to start the colouring and he was looking at the ceiling with an expression that was somewhere between angry and bored. I looked away as quickly as I could before he felt my eyes on him. It was the longest hour of my life and all the time I was willing someone else to come in the studio: maybe Gary might come by even though it was his day off...

Of course, no-one came.

Somehow I managed to finish the tattoo with clean lines and no mistakes. When I got out the tub of Vaseline the man sniggered and my face burned crimson.

'It helps it to heal cleanly,' I mumbled.

I gritted my teeth, applied a smear of jelly across the new tattoo and taped a piece of cling film over it. Something vengeful in me deliberately put the sticky tape over his hairy thigh.

He jumped up off the couch and pulled his trousers up. I thrust a photocopied aftercare leaflet into his hand. Normal protocol would be to explain all the important points – keep the tattoo dry, don't scratch it whilst it heals – but I needed him to be gone as quickly as possible.

'That'll be forty pounds please.'

'No.'

'But...'

'You've got a cheek, haven't you? The thing is I've got this problem. Somebody has taken something of mine, and I need it back. Urgently. Billy knows where it is but he's fucked up and can't tell me. So on account of me being a nice guy I'll come back another time, and when I do you'd better have remembered where it is. OK?'

The door slammed behind him. I staggered across the studio and fumbled and pushed the bolt back into the loose hasp. Then I ran to the back room and shut that door, too.

I sat down at the table and the realisation hit me that I couldn't work like this any more, I couldn't deal with the idea that this guy might come back. Who was he? I fled to the outhouse and threw up my lunch in the newly scrubbed toilet.

I leant, shaking and gagging, over the pan. Maybe if I asked Gary he would let me do all the female clients from now on and run special sessions for women on the days I was here on my own. It had to be worth trying.

Chapter Fifteen

December 1993

I didn't sleep that night and I spent the next day at work watching the door; when Gary asked if I was expecting someone, I made up an excuse about a friend who said they might come in to check out some designs, and then I hid in the back room, claiming a headache. I wondered about telling him about the stranger yesterday but there was no point, there was nothing he could do.

I felt like a nervous wreck: exhausted and drained of energy. I couldn't bear another sleepless night and needed something to take the edge off my anxiety, so at lunchtime I went to see Maggie to score.

As I lingered outside her shop, deciding whether or not to go in, she looked through the window and caught my eye.

'Hi.' I felt unaccountably guilty.

'Are you alright, pet?'

'Yeah, it's all good...just a bit...you know.' I gestured vaguely with my hands and tried to smile.

She gave me a look that felt as if she was peering into my soul. 'No it's not. Come inside, I'll put the kettle on.'

'I'm fine, really I am.'

She ignored my protestations and gestured me through the door. My legs felt powerless and I followed her in.

'Tea?'

'Please.'

I sat at the folding table in the back of her shop and she served us a builder-strong brew in dainty floral cups.

'So, what's the matter?'

I felt tears start to prickle at the backs of my eyes. 'Oh – it's…it's…everything,' I said and started to cry.

Maggie put a sturdy hand on my shoulder and listened to me as I wept about Sullivan's desertion and Siobhan, Billy's breakdown, my abortion. I left out any mention about the stranger yesterday though: Maggie would ask too many questions that I couldn't face answering.

'Oh, you poor thing,' she said when I finally ran out of words. 'You've kept all this bottled up, haven't you?'

'Oh Maggie,' I sniffed. 'You don't know the half of it. Can you do my cards or read my hand again for me? I feel like I'm lost and can't find my way home; I don't know what to do.'

She shook her head. 'You're too upset for me to do a reading now, it won't work. Come back in a week or two though, and we'll do it properly. But what I can tell you is that Siobhan is a five-minute piece of nonsense. She'll have had enough of him in a month or two and move on.'

'And when she's left him, will he come back to me?' I asked. The thought of Siobhan leaving Sullivan made my heart leap.

'You don't want him back, even if he asks you,' said Maggie. 'Trust me, he's a weak man, he always will be; the ones like that never change. Let him go, you can do so much better.'

I nodded in mute agreement.

'He'd never have been a good father, either. Some men, it brings out the best in them, but he isn't one of them. He wouldn't have coped with being second best.'

'How can you tell all that?' I said, but Maggie only looked at me and smiled.

'Maggie, can I come to see you at home later? I need to score. I'm not sleeping; I'm so stressed all the time...'

'I've got exactly the thing.'

She rummaged in the big Welsh dresser at the back of the shop and gave me a small plastic packet full of what looked like dried leaves.

'Try this, pet. It's a herbal sleeping remedy,' she said. 'Boil two teaspoons of it up in a mug of water to make tea and drink it – all of it – last thing at night.'

'Is it safe?'

'Oh, of course it is, it's just herbs. Now, you've enough there for a few days. Give it a try and let me know how you get on.'

'How much do I owe you?'

'Don't be daft. It's on the house.'

I boiled up some of the mixture that night. It smelt vile and tasted worse, but for the first time since Baildon I slept for nine hours straight and didn't have a single bad dream.

When I went back to see Maggie, I felt better than I had in ages.

'I wanted to say thank you.'

'Ah, good. It worked then?'

'I slept like a baby – it must've been the first time in months I didn't have nightmares. What was in that stuff?'

She smiled and tapped the side of her nose. 'That's my little secret, I'm afraid.'

'Thanks. Um, can you do that tarot reading for me please? I feel so much better, but I still don't know what to do.'

I sat at the same folding table – now covered with a green velvet shawl – and watched Maggie shuffle the tarot deck. The cards looked ancient; the gold patterns on the backs were smudged and grey with years of use.

'Take a card.'

I felt a terrible sense of responsibility – what if I chose the wrong one? Indecision paralysed me until Maggie looked at me with concern over her half-moon glasses.

'I can't,' I said.

She spread the deck on the table and took three cards from it seemingly at random. She told me what each one signified: that I'd been let down by someone close, I'd been through a great upheaval, but that things would start to look up very soon.

'How soon?'

She gazed at the cards and tapped at the Queen of Wands. 'There's a big change coming in the New Year,' she said. 'It'll need a lot of hard work – there always is with change, if you're to make the best of it – but you'll reap the rewards for a long time if you put your mind to it.'

I shook my head. The betrayal aside – which she knew already – her reading didn't sound like my life at all.

I spent Christmas morning rattling around the flat feeling desperately lonely. The empty day yawned ahead of me and every five minutes dragged like an hour. I tried watching television but after ten minutes of *It's A Wonderful Life*, I felt even worse. I went for a walk but it was sleeting: I was soaked and freezing by the time I'd got halfway round the block.

I hadn't bought any groceries – unable to admit to myself that it was only me to shop for I'd put it off until it was too late – so my lunch was cornflakes and a slice of toast.

I thought about calling Barbara to wish her a Happy Christmas, but couldn't bring myself to pick up the phone. Sullivan would have told her by now that we'd split up and I worried what she'd think if I phoned up out of the blue. I thought he'd probably told her it was all my fault; maybe he'd even taken Siobhan home for the holidays.

I toyed with the idea of calling Simon and Annette or maybe Rob so I could hear a friendly voice but I didn't know what to say. For a brief, desperate moment I even considered phoning my own parents but I pushed that idea away as quickly as it came.

After an hour staring at the phone I went back to the hospital to see Billy: I had to get out the flat and thought the drive would do me good. For what it was worth I bought him a box of chocolates and a Christmas card from the petrol station. Outside the city the roads were deserted and I didn't see a single other car: the drive to Menston felt as if the world had ended.

The hospital loomed against the grey sky and looked more unwelcoming than ever; the tired decorations at Reception did nothing to help. I popped my head around the door of Billy's room but he was asleep, so I put the card and chocolates on his bedside locker and tiptoed out so as not to disturb him. I couldn't help but notice there was a card from his mum – a cartoon of Santa and plump reindeer – but there was nothing from Sullivan.

PART TWO

Chapter Sixteen

December 1993-February 1994

After Christmas I somehow found the strength to move out of the West Bowling flat. It felt dead and empty without Sullivan and no longer home; just a collection of unbearable memories.

I forced myself to dump the last of his belongings – a pair of old jeans that were torn and flapping at the knees, some dirty socks I found under the bed, a packet of guitar strings – in the bin. Packing felt impossibly hard; every bag and box a reminder of what had happened and proof that Sullivan was never coming back.

I thought about telling him that I'd moved, but there was no point. I re-addressed all his mail to Simon and Annette's, shoved it in the nearest post box and hoped he'd get the hint.

I gritted my teeth, loaded everything I owned into the Wreck and moved to an attic bedsit in a dead-end crescent on the opposite side of Bradford. The irony of its location overlooking the cemetery did not escape me.

Once I'd moved I couldn't bear to keep the Land Rover any more: every time I drove it I thought of Rudy, dead on the back seat and with his head bouncing against the window as we drove over the moors. I sold it for cash to a no-questions-asked dealer in a sheepskin coat and I didn't even argue when he offered me half of what it was worth.

One evening I felt so furious at everything that had happened, I pulled my long fuchsia hair into a high ponytail and hacked the lot off with the kitchen scissors. I burst into tears as soon as I saw what I'd done, the clumps of pink lying scattered on the floor.

'Been dumped have you, love?' asked the hairdresser as she looked at my handiwork after I'd slunk into her salon, a woolly hat pulled down over my ears to hide the butchered remains of my hair. 'Don't worry, it happens all the time. What did he do, leave you for another girl?'

'Yeah.'

She tidied it up into an elfin crop and I asked her to dye the whole lot brown at the same time. I hardly recognised myself when she'd finished.

By the time Monday morning rolled round I couldn't wait to get out of my lonely bedsit and back to work. I was in the studio with the kettle on by a quarter to nine.

'I'm selling up,' said Gary when he came in. He wouldn't look me in the eye. 'The missus, she doesn't like Bradford, never has done, and she's always on at me for us to go back to Clitheroe. Well, we had a long talk over Christmas and she's ready to move back to her mother's if I don't go along with it. So I'm going to have to let you go, Julia. It's a shame and I'll be sad to see you go; don't get me wrong, you've been a good worker. I'll pay you what you're due and an extra week's wages.'

I felt as if the floor was about to swallow me. Work was the only thing I had to keep me going these days; I couldn't cope with the thought of Gary leaving me too.

'How much do you want?' The words fell out of my mouth.

'You what?'

'For the lease on this place, I'll take it over and run it…I'll take on another junior and…'

'Are you sure? I've never heard of a lass running her own place before.'

'I'm sure,' I said.

He named an amount that was half of what was left of Rudy's money. I knew he was probably ripping me off but before I could change my mind about what I was doing, I went home and stuffed the cash into an old envelope.

I ran all the way back to work down the Otley Road, the frigid air burning my lungs with every breath, irrationally convinced that everyone knew what I was carrying.

I leant on the counter and tried to catch my breath. Sweat ran down my neck and my shirt was stuck to my back. I pulled the envelope from my inside pocket. 'Here you are; it's all there. Count it if you like.'

Gary looked at me, at the envelope full of notes and back at me again. 'Bloody hell, love,' he said at last. 'You're serious. What did you do, rob a bank?'

'Someone died and left it to me.'

When Gary took the money to the bank in the afternoon I suddenly remembered what Sullivan had said about only spending a bit of it at a time and I paced up and down the studio, biting my fingernails and dreading the phone call to say there was something wrong with the money, that the notes were stolen, that the serial numbers didn't match...

I pounced on Gary the moment he came back. 'Was everything alright?'

'Piece of cake,' he said, and whistled to himself for the rest of the day.

It was obvious Gary couldn't wait to leave because I'd never seen him so cheerful in all the time we'd worked together. He talked about opening another tattoo parlour back in Clitheroe, and told me how he'd already made an offer on a shop near the castle.

A month later the studio was all mine, and the day after Gary left, I stood in the shop and looked at the battered lino and the dusty sheets of flash on greying walls and wondered what I was going to do with it. It was if I was seeing the place with new eyes: it was dank and depressing and needed a complete overhaul.

As I tidied up I began to have serious second thoughts about what I'd done. How on earth could I manage the place on my own? Perhaps Gary had a point; maybe there was a good reason that women didn't run their own studios. The thought of single-handedly dealing with an endless parade of male clients filled me with loathing. I knew I didn't want more of the same: dodgy customers wanting cheap flash: hearts and skulls and Harleys. What I wanted was a studio that did high-quality tattoos with distinctive designs: something different, something unique.

An idea began to form as I sorted through Gary's piles of paperwork.

I turned Gary's run-down tattoo parlour into The Yellow Room: Bradford's first and only women-only tattooists, with vanilla scented candles, daffodil paint and heavy primrose drapes. I bought a reproduction Louis XIV desk from the flea market to replace the old reception counter and sanded and stained it and topped it off with a vase of artificial sunflowers.

I worked like a demon and put in sixteen and eighteen hour days of non-stop physical labour – scrubbing, painting, varnishing – so I didn't have time to think about what I was doing. I took out an advert in the local paper announcing the re-opening and advertised for an assistant in a trade magazine. *Experienced tattoo artist required for innovative new women-only West Yorkshire studio. Must have own portfolio. No timewasters. Please call for more details.*

I had three phone calls: a young man with no experience bar tattooing his mates, a woman who did nothing but fairies and angels, and Esme.

Esme was twenty-one, fresh out of Art College and as keen as a knife: she was the only one of the three I bothered to interview. Even over the phone I knew she was exactly right for what I had in mind, and when she told me she never did walk-up clients without a proper consultation we hit it off straight away.

We met for an informal chat over a cup of coffee in the half-finished studio; the tang of white spirit was thick in the air. After I looked at her portfolio – a ring binder packed with perfect examples of everything from intricate Japanese dot-work to fashionable Celtic knots to classic designs – I hired her on the spot. With her long red curls she bore a resemblance to Lizzie Siddal, if Rosetti's muse had worn embroidered Levis and had rings in her eyebrows.

Chapter Seventeen

February-May 1994

The Yellow Room officially opened on a Wednesday lunchtime. The smell of new paint and antiseptic hung in the air and watery spring sunshine seeped through the yellow curtains. Clannad played on the stereo and we toasted the occasion with a pot of tea.

'It's beautiful,' said Esme as she looked around.

'It is, isn't it?' I said. I felt strange – not frightened exactly; just slightly nervous and happy at the same time. It took several hours for me to realise I was excited.

We had one customer that first day; an old client of Gary's who I'd postponed until after the refurbishment. The next day and the day after that no-one came at all.

On the Saturday we had a hen party arrive; down from Harrogate in a flurry of tiaras and L-plates, drunk on Lambrusco and chattering like parakeets. They clamoured into the studio, pointing out designs to each other and shrieking with laughter. We gently shooed them away and told them to come back when they were sober.

'We'll give you a ten percent discount!' I said as they left, but I wasn't hopeful in the slightest that they would return. I tried to ignore the doubt that was starting to nibble at the back of my mind.

'Do you want another cuppa?' asked Esme. It must have been the fifth cup of tea that we'd had that day: despite the fact it was Thursday our second client of the week had not long left. There was nothing else for us to do: I'd already cleaned all the surfaces and re-filed our paperwork twice.

'Thanks.' I slumped into the fat cream sofa and put my head in my hands. The familiar feeling of dread was tugging at me again and I felt exhausted.

'It's not going to work is it?' I said. 'I've been so stupid – what use is a women-only tattoo studio? I've excluded ninety percent of our clients before we've even started. Oh Esme, what have I done?'

'It's only early days yet,' she said.

'Hmmm.' I envied her enthusiasm – and her confidence in me.

'Why don't we get some flyers done, Ju? The print shop by the post office has got a special deal on if you get five hundred.'

She was right. We spent the rest of the day designing advertisements and in desperation I got a thousand full-colour leaflets printed. We took turns to hand them out around town – in pubs, at clubs, in independent record shops, outside both train stations and all over the Student Union. The customers finally started to trickle in, but more than once I was thankful for Rudy's money: it was the only thing that kept the Yellow Room afloat those first few weeks.

One afternoon Esme took a phone call from the journalist Janie Ross. Janie didn't want a tattoo though; instead she booked a two-hour slot to interview us about our exclusive women-only business. We thought it was a hoax at first but she explained that her PA had picked up one of our flyers on a visit to her sister and Janie, scenting an opportunity for a story, had got on the phone.

'Why on earth does she want to talk to us?' Esme said after she'd put the phone down. 'We're just a little back-street studio in Bradford. Surely there must be other women-only tattooists around?'

I shrugged. 'I've no idea.'

Janie arrived wearing her trademark white fun-fur coat, red lipstick and Jackie O sunglasses – taller in real life than on the television, and greyhound-thin. We stammered, awe-struck, into her Dictaphone with some spur of the moment nonsense about making a political statement through our work, and we flushed with embarrassment when her photographer made us pose for pictures.

When the interview was done Esme had the cheek to offer Janie a fifty percent discount if she made a booking, but she declined graciously in that lazy Australian drawl of hers.

After they left Esme and I stared at each other in disbelief.

'Pinch me,' I said to her. 'Am I dreaming?'

She shook her head and looked bemused. 'We have just been interviewed by the one and only Janie Ross, haven't we?'

'We have, and apparently we're subverting the patriarchal society through the medium of body art. Isn't that what you said?'

'Oh God, did I?'

We giggled at each other and retired to the back room for celebratory tea and chocolate digestives.

Our advertising campaign kept things ticking over to the point I no longer had to bolster our takings with Rudy's money. Six new clients booked appointments after seeing our flyers, and we had our first repeat customer too.

I didn't think any more about the interview but a few weeks later Janie sent us a charming handwritten note, thanking us for our time and wishing us luck with our venture. Accompanying the letter was a copy of the glossy Sunday colour supplement that she wrote for.

Her article – full of enthusiastic praise for the Yellow Room, our unique designs and our underpinning principles – was spread across the centre pages under the headline "Are These Women the Future of British Feminism?"

The photo alongside the article showed the two of us sitting side by side on the sofa, Esme's red curls framing her face like a halo whilst I looked every inch the indie rock star, dressed from head to foot in black and with my growing-out crop flopping over one eye. We framed the pages for a laugh and hung them on the wall next to the gilt Victorian mirror.

On the Monday morning the phone began to ring as soon as we opened and it never seemed to stop. By the end of the summer we were both working fifty hours a week to keep up with demand, and there was still a month-long waiting list.

We had clients arrive from all over the country and beyond; one woman even came over especially from France. I bought a map and put it on the wall; we stuck coloured pins in it to show where all our customers came from.

One day Esme came back from lunch – a rarity now, since Janie's article – clutching a new CD.

'Do you mind if I play this?' she said and put the disc into our hi-fi system.

Even if the opening bars of the first track hadn't been so familiar I would have recognised the singer's voice anywhere. I gasped and thought I was going to pass out from the shock.

'Turn it off!'

Esme looked as though I'd slapped her. 'Oh bloody hell, sorry Ju.'

'Was that Sydenham Poyntz?'

'Wow, you've heard of them? Yeah, they're great aren't they, you know that DJ on Radio 1 who does all the unsigned bands on the midnight sessions? He's always playing the same two songs by these guys over and over, he reckons they're the best band since The Undertones and now thanks to him they've got an album out, and there's a tour and everything...here, are you all right? You've gone ever so pale.'

I sat down heavily and rubbed my eyes. 'Yeah, I'm fine. It's just weird hearing them again.'

'Weird? Why's that?'

'Oh, it's nothing; I used to know them years ago. We...we were at uni together.'

She squealed. 'Oh my God, you know them? And what about the lead singer – isn't he absolutely *gorgeous*?'

I forced out a sickly noise that wasn't quite a laugh.

'Sullivan? Yes, I suppose he was.'

New Musical Express, 27 July 1996

Sydenham Poyntz Reading Show Cancelled:

Bassist Reportedly Still "Unwell" Following Germany Incident

Rockers Sydenham Poyntz have confirmed longstanding rumours that they will no longer appear at this year's Reading Festival.

Booked to perform on the NME stage alongside Rocket from the Crypt and Screaming Trees, Sydenham Poyntz mysteriously dropped from view following bassist Simon Gray's widely reported dramatic onstage meltdown in Germany in February.

"Simon still isn't fully recovered," said front man and founding member Sullivan. "The doctors have advised him to rest and cut down on commitments for at least six months. We're very sad to let down our fans like this but the band all wish Simon the best for a speedy recovery and we hope to be back on the road and back in the recording studio soon."

The announcement was made on Tuesday following rumours in the music press that the band was on indefinite hiatus.

Gray was recently photographed by a fan outside his home, looking gaunt and confused, and the resulting scuffle led to rumours that he was suffering from drug and alcohol problems.

Sydenham Poyntz's as yet unnamed third album is pencilled for release in early 1997.

Yorkshire Life, March 1997

Bradford's Yellow Room: Yorkshire's Women-Only Tattoo Studio

The Yellow Room tattoo studio in Bradford, West Yorkshire must surely be the only one of its kind. Run in partnership by Julia Cox (*right, opposite*) and Esme Brennan, the studio has been offering "high-class art tattoos by women, for women" for the past three years. They were recently awarded the Yorkshire Small Business Award and *Yorkshire Life* went along to find out more.

Yorkshire Life: How did you come up with the idea of a female-friendly studio?

Julia: I founded the studio in 1994: I'd been working in the business since leaving university and then had the opportunity to take over the studio as my own. I wanted to move away from the usual cliché of dodgy backstreet parlours churning out the same uninspiring designs. It seemed a perfect chance to follow my heart and do something I'd always wanted.

Esme: A lot of women don't feel comfortable getting tattooed in an all-male environment – most of our clients come here to get away from that sort of thing.

YL: The Yellow Room doesn't look like your average tattoo studio.

J: *(Laughs)*. That was the idea, to make it look as welcoming and friendly as we could, and as unlike your typical tattooist's as possible.

E: So we have the miniature chandeliers and fairy lights, the candelabra and the bird cage in the window, the vintage furniture...

YL: Why did you decide to call it the Yellow Room?

J: It's named after the feminist short story *The Yellow Wallpaper* – it was written in 1892 about a woman's confinement in a room with yellow wallpaper and her descent into madness at the hands of her controlling husband. It seemed to fit with our philosophy at the time.

YL: How did it feel to win the Bradford Best Small Business award?

J: It was fantastic, the absolute icing on the cake: such a great honour to be recognised in my adopted town. I'm still in shock; it's such a huge privilege to be nominated for the award, let alone to win. To be honest it hasn't quite sunk in yet.

YL: Tell us some more about your business ethos.

J: When I started the Yellow Room I wanted to do something different. Not only to make the studio exclusively for women, but to make sure each piece we do is unique. Sure, we have a portfolio of standard designs but we encourage our customers to adapt a design to their own requirements: that might be the colours, shading, or combining elements of a couple of different pieces to fit with what the customer wants.

E: We insist that every client has a consultation before committing to the actual tattoo.

We don't do walk-ups – that's clients who come in off the street and want a tattoo there and then – our customers must come for the consultation first. We usually schedule that a couple of weeks beforehand, although we can plan it as a single appointment if it's needed. We are very strict about that, and it means that the client has the opportunity to be involved in the design process and to customise the tattoo to meet their individual needs.

YL: What are your secrets for running a successful tattoo business?

J: We use organic inks. They're more expensive than the traditional pigments but the colours stay truer for longer: things like the purples and greens are much more vivid and long-lasting. We import ours from Canada.

E: Proper aftercare is the secret to a good tattoo, so instead of using Vaseline, we prefer fair-trade South American cocoa butter. It helps speed up the healing process, meaning the tattoo is less likely to scab and be damaged – and it smells lovely, too.

The Yellow Room, 16 Thursby Street, Bradford, West Yorkshire BD3 9DY. Tel/fax 01274 969655. Open Monday to Saturday 11am-7pm, Sundays by prior appointment. Prices (including a one-hour consultation) start from £75 for two hours.

Melody Maker

14 March 1998

Sydenham Poyntz Announce Split

Bradford band Sydenham Poyntz formally announced their split this week, following a two-year hiatus.

In a press release the band said that they have decided to go their separate ways due to musical differences.

"After ten years of recording and performing together, the band have been on pause for a period whilst we consider our future directions," the statement from their record label read.

"We have come to realise that although we have the greatest love and respect for each other our energies will be better directed towards solo efforts and other collaborations."

Members of the band were unavailable for comment as *Melody Maker* went to press.

Tattoo Monthly, June 2000
Winner of the 2000 British Tattoo Association Award Announced

The Yellow Room – the UK's first women-only studio – has been announced as the winner of the British Tattoo Association's 2000 award for Best Studio.

Opened in 1994 by artists Julia Cox (*left in photo*), and Esme Brennan, the quirky Bradford studio, complete with vintage furniture and chandeliers, sees around twenty clients a week, many of whom return time and again, attracted by their strict ladies-only policy. Another of the Yellow Room's unique selling points is their requirement that all clients book for a full consultation in advance. As a result they strive to ensure that each client's individual needs and wishes are taken into account during the creative process.

"This is such an honour," said Julia when interviewed by *Tattoo Monthly*. "I'd like to thank everyone who nominated our little studio; I can't begin to describe how much this means to Esme and me."

Q Magazine

March 2004

Distant Thunder – Sydenham Poyntz

Disappointing third album from a band who keep on going - perhaps they shouldn't.

Who would have guessed that Bradford indie outfit Sydenham Poyntz would make a comeback? The departure of three of the four founding members – leaving front man Sullivan to continue alone with a hastily-assembled Sydenham Poyntz Version 2 – means the band are now only a shadow of their mid-90s selves. Their much-awaited third album could have been an occasion to celebrate, but *Distant Thunder* is not melodically blessed and ultimately this 12-track LP is about ten songs too long.

The Hunter has a certain robust charm and *Outer Space* is a half decent pop number, but when they break out the cloying ballads it becomes impossible to care any more.

●○○○○

Mojo

June 2006

Obituary: Simon Gray (1970-2006)

Born in Canvey Island, Essex – famously the home of 1970s R&B outfit Dr Feelgood – Simon Gray was best known as a founding member of 90s rockers Sydenham Poyntz.

The band was formed in 1988 when 18-year old Gray met lead singer Jeremy Sullivan at university; Gray co-wrote lyrics and contributed bass guitar duties to the band's first two albums.

Following an onstage collapse in Germany in 1996 – which was widely rumoured at the time to be drug-related – he left the band to work on other, as yet unreleased, projects.

The Bradford-based musician was found dead at his home on 5 April this year from an overdose of prescription drugs.

At the time of his death he had recently been discharged from a court-ordered addiction treatment programme, following a series of convictions for theft and heroin and crack cocaine possession.

Gray is survived by his partner and their four-year old daughter.

None of the surviving members of Sydenham Poyntz were available for comment as *Mojo* went to press.

The Huddersfield Examiner

19 July 2010

Sydenham Poyntz at The Hall Inn, Sowerby Bridge

Sydenham Poyntz aren't from Sydenham, London – they're from Bradford, and there are three new members in the rebooted line up of this once-successful Nineties band.

The outfit is fronted by founding member Sullivan, now supported by three up-and-coming local musicians.

They performed two songs from the 2004 album *Distant Thunder* and a handful of older tracks.

There were a few high moments, notably with an up-tempo cover of the perennial Doors favourite *People Are Strange*; but sad to say Sydenham Poyntz failed to set the night on fire.

Q Magazine

May 2012

"Where Are They Now?"

Jon McGough from Gosport, Hampshire asks: where are Sydenham Poyntz now?

When their first album *Honesty* charted in mid-1994, with catchy tunes and barbed, socially aware lyrics, Sydenham Poyntz promised to be one of the UK's hottest new bands. It seemed evident that, overnight sensation status notwithstanding, the indie/alt rock foursome was here to stay. Except they were anything but overnight sensations, having toured the Leeds and Bradford circuit for several years, and were already falling apart.

Formed by Jeremy Sullivan (vocals, lead guitar) and Simon Gray (bass) at Bradford University in the late 1980s, Sydenham Poyntz's first album hit the top spot in the indie charts and number 6 in the Top 40 in the weeks following its release. Championed by the sorely missed maverick DJ Dave Rook, they seemed destined for great things, but internal tensions and subsequent multiple line-up changes meant the band never recreated the success of their first release.

Original drummer Rob Kelly's current whereabouts are currently unknown but he is believed to be living in the London area and retired from the music business.

Jason Rose (rhythm guitar) now works as a music teacher and manages a successful guitar shop in his home town of Rhyl, North Wales.

Following Gray's sudden and dramatic departure from the band due to health problems midway through their 1996 European tour to promote their second album *The Wages of War*, he retired from live performance and focussed on personal projects. At the time of his death from an overdose of alcohol and prescription sleeping pills in early 2006, aged only 36, he was working on a self-produced album of classic rock and roll standards.

Sullivan still continues to tour occasionally with a new line-up following the original Sydenham Poyntz's implosion. He tells *Q* that the band is planning to head back to the studio next year to lay down tracks for a new album, their first release since 2004's critically panned LP *Distant Thunder*.

Chapter Eighteen

September 2013

I'm sitting at the desk in the back room sorting through piles of receipts and invoices, ready for a meeting with the accountants on Friday. Esme is finishing up in the main studio, washing the floor and prepping for the next day's clients. She's got the radio on and I can hear her singing along to a Kaiser Chiefs' song as she cleans; it makes me smile despite the heaps of paper on the table and the autumn rain hammering against the windows.

'I'm off now Ju,' she says, putting her head round the door to the office. 'Don't work too late.'

'I promise. See you tomorrow.'

The bell on the door chimes as Esme walks into the wet Bradford evening. I look at my watch, it's only six o'clock but after an afternoon of admin it feels much later. I yawn and stand up to stretch the muscles in my back; my shoulders ache from being hunched over the desk. I need some more caffeine to get me through the next hour, when all the paperwork will be done and I can finally go home. I spoon coffee into my mug and rub my eyes whilst I wait for the kettle to boil.

The bell rings again and footsteps squeak across the lino.

'Hiya,' I call out.

There's no reply so I go into the studio and there is a man standing there. He's clean-shaven and smartly dressed in an expensive-looking overcoat and cashmere scarf. He's big and solidly built, around six feet tall, and he looks vaguely familiar – there is something about his eyes – but I can't quite place him.

'Can I help you?'

'Yes. I think you can.'

Prickles of fear run up my neck and I swallow and try to smile. 'How can I help?'

He stares at me as if he recognises me from somewhere too, and I see that his hands are shaking. I step to one side – a step closer to the back room – to try and put some space between us.

'I said I think you can.'

'I'm sorry, I don't...?'

He stands at the front desk with his hands spread across the top. He looks around.

'It's a nice place you've got here.'

'Th...thanks.'

'You're famous, Julia. You've had your picture in magazines, they even printed your address and phone number. You were the easy one to find.'

'I don't understand. What do you want?'

He smiles but it doesn't reach his eyes and it only highlights his brittleness. The man reaches into the inside pocket of his overcoat and pulls out some photographs. He takes two long strides towards me and pushes the photos in my face. His breath is as sour as stale milk and the smell makes me reflexively step back.

'Do you recognise these?'

One of the pictures is of Rudy at a family gathering: Rudy, someone I assume is his brother and their parents, standing in a suburban garden on a sunny day. Everyone is dressed in formal clothes, as if for a wedding. The second photo is of the farmhouse, with Rudy framed by the front door and squinting into the sun. I look at the first picture again and realise with a surging sense of horror that the man in front of me is Martin Baxter.

'You know what happened to my brother.'

I look him in the face. Long-buried scenes of Baildon flash in my mind's eye like a kaleidoscope: the three of us in Rudy's filthy bedroom, Sullivan and I playing pool in the pub, Tina running to the bathroom to be sick.

'I have no idea what you're talking about.'

'Yes you do. Your friend Billy helped the police discredit my brother, and that is why he's locked up in Lynfield Mount. Tell me the truth!'

His words fade and I'm no longer in the Yellow Room: my mind has spun back to where all of this started and I'm standing at the kitchen sink in the farmhouse in my underwear, filling a mug with water because my head is pounding from drinking too much whisky. The pipes are thundering and Rudy's hands are in my knickers and around my throat, and I think I'm going to die.

I'm paralysed. My brain is telling me to fight, to lash out and hit him but I can't do it, held back by the knowledge of what would happen if I did: I have a vivid mental picture of Martin lying dead on the floor of the studio, his skull crushed against the antique reception desk, blood pooling on the tiles and no sign of a pulse.

'Tell me the truth!'

Anger is simmering in me like boiling fat and I explode. I grab a tattoo machine – the only thing within reach – and point it at him like a gun.

'You've got five seconds to get out before I call the police.'

Martin stares at me; he is breathing so hard his nostrils flare. I stare him in the eye and will him to go.

'One...two...'

'You haven't heard the last of this.'

'Three.'

My right arm is still raised, the machine's brushed steel grip clenched in my shaking hand. The machine is disconnected and empty, the needle removed: it might look threatening but in fact it's useless.

'I said get out!'

We stare at each other for another long second and without breaking my gaze I move towards the phone.

'Four!'

Martin runs out the door and disappears down the street.

I put the tattoo machine back on the desk with quivering hands; it feels so small and fragile now. My palms are clammy and I'm afraid I'll drop it. The world turns muffled and dark, and a sudden burst of sweat runs down my face. I clutch onto the desk for support and take a deep breath but it's no good: my legs give way and I fall down, landing on my knees on the black-and-white floor. I'm suddenly bone-weary so I rest there on my hands and knees with my face pressed against the side of the desk waiting for the feeling to pass, dimly aware that I've fainted but so out of it that I don't care.

After a few minutes – or it might be longer because time doesn't have any meaning any more – I'm hazily aware of someone calling my name from somewhere a long way away.

'Oh my God, what's going on? Ju, what's the matter?'

Esme helps me stand up; my legs are useless and feel as if they are made of rubber. She helps me to the back room and makes me a mug of milky coffee with far too much sugar, telling me it's for the shock and I find that don't have the energy to argue. She sits with me to make sure I drink all of it, but I insist that she locks the front door first.

'God, I only came back because I forgot my purse. What happened?'

I can't tell her the truth. 'Some bloke showed up – he threatened me...'

'We should phone the police.' She takes her mobile from her handbag.

'No!'

Esme looks taken aback and slightly afraid.

'Sorry – I didn't mean to shout.'

'Why on earth not?' She chews her lip. 'Was it someone you know?'

I say the first thing that comes into my head. 'He was angry because his wife had a tattoo done. She...she booked in on your day off last week...she got a Green Man done on her shoulder and he wants to sue me, says she's disfigured herself.'

She gasps. 'Bloody hell, what a twat.'

'Yeah, I told him to get out.'

'What if he comes back?'

'I don't think he will but I'll phone the police tomorrow. It's not urgent any more.'

'His poor wife. We'll keep the door locked from now on,' says Esme. Her lips are thin and pursed and her eyes are flashing: she's angry and frightened on my behalf. 'It's not as though we do walk-ups, is it? We'll put a sign up telling people to ring the doorbell.'

I'm only half listening but I nod and agree with her whilst I sip my coffee. I feel cold to the bone, shivering as if I'm coming down with a fever and my knees are beginning to sting and throb as the adrenaline wears off. I hold the mug with both hands, afraid I'll spill it otherwise.

'What's Lynfield Mount?'

'You what? It's the mental hospital.'

'You're kidding?'

'Why'd you ask?'

'He said something about it – said I belonged there.'

'Here,' said Esme. 'Do you reckon he's a patient and he's escaped or something?'

I try to laugh but it doesn't work and I start crying instead. 'I don't know; I really don't know.'

'Oh, Ju. You're shock. Come on, let me take you home.'

Esme insists on seeing me in the front door. I'm freezing and exhausted and feel as if I could sleep for a fortnight.

'Take the day off tomorrow,' she says. 'I can manage on my own.'

'Thanks.'

'Are you sure you'll be alright? I can stay the night if you like.'

'It's fine. Thanks for offering but I'll be OK.'

We go inside and I turn all the lights on in the lounge.

'Hang on a sec,' I say and drag myself upstairs, suddenly and irrationally convinced that Martin has somehow got into the house. I check the bedroom and bathroom, pulling back the shower curtain and opening the wardrobe.

Esme knows what I'm doing and without saying anything she switches on the light over the back door, illuminating the rockery and making shadows leap up the wall. She goes outside, turns on the flashlight on her phone and shines it around the dark corners of the yard.

'You're all right,' she says. 'He's not here.'

'Sorry – it's crazy I know, but he said he knew where I lived.' I shiver again.

'Are you sure you don't want to stay at my place tonight?'

'I'm fine, I'm just being silly.'

When at last I have convinced Esme that I really will be safe on my own, I double lock the front door and soak in a hot bubble bath. I lock the bathroom door too, and take my mobile phone with me: I feel vulnerable and exposed, as if I've lost a layer of skin.

Purple bruises are beginning to blossom on my knees where I collapsed. I wrap myself in a fluffy towel and try to make sense of everything that's happened this evening. Has Martin been to see Sullivan? What did he mean about Billy being "locked up in Lynfield Mount"?

I haven't thought about Billy for a long time. I assumed that he had got over his breakdown and had been discharged from hospital; perhaps living quietly with his mum or round the corner from Sullivan: maybe he'd even gone back to uni. I haven't seen him for years, and it makes me sad trying to think where the time has gone. I'm too tired to think of any answers right now and the idea of trying to explain everything to Sullivan fills me with panicky dread.

I'm flagging again so I fill a hot water bottle and go to bed. Marwood jumps on the bed beside me where he nuzzles my ear, kneads industriously at the quilt and eventually purrs us both to sleep.

In the middle of the night a strange noise disturbs me and I wake with a start. I switch on the light and blink in the brightness, holding my breath and waiting for the noise again.

'Marwood? Marwood, is that you?'

There is a soft thump from downstairs. I pull on my dressing gown and turn all the lights on before stiffly making my way down to the living room: the wooden landing floor is cold under my feet and the ache in my knees is a painful reminder of yesterday's confrontation. I think about grabbing something I to defend myself but there's nothing in the bedroom I can use.

Of course, when I get downstairs there is nobody there: only Marwood sitting on the table, washing his ears and wearing an expression of angelic innocence despite the glass candlestick lying in shards in the fireplace.

I check the doors and windows while I try to ignore the fear that's hammering in my chest. Maybe I should get a burglar alarm installed, have bars put over the kitchen window to stop anyone coming in the back…I take a dustpan and brush from the cupboard and sweep up the shattered candlestick. My heart is still thudding and I peer through the front and back curtains, expecting to see a figure outside, watching and waiting.

As dawn breaks I hear footsteps along the street but it's only a neighbour: a man who I slightly know by sight, muffled against the cold in a maroon fleece. A few minutes later a woman comes out from the house two doors down and waits in the street with her laptop case and handbag until a yellow sports car pulls up; she waves to the driver and gets inside.

I mentally check off the cars that are parked along the street, some are familiar to me but many aren't; it reminds me how isolated my cottage is a quarter of a mile from the main road and in a quiet back street where I only know two of the neighbours. I look again and notice there is a dark blue Mercedes parked at the end of the road. I don't recognise it and I'm utterly convinced that it belongs to Martin Baxter.

The thought of the car – and of Martin waiting there for me – makes me feel even more edgy and restless. I don't want to stay at home all day so I feed Marwood and get dressed. My car is still at the Yellow Room so I call a cab to get to work; whilst I wait for it to arrive I lock the back door and check three times that the windows are fastened shut.

When the taxi pulls away I force myself to look out the back window at the Mercedes, but it's empty.

Chapter Nineteen

September 2013

'Ju! What are you doing here? I thought you were taking the day off.'

'I'm fine,' I say but I don't feel it. 'There's no point in moping around at home. Anyway, the accounts won't do themselves.'

'You're being really brave, you know.'

'Am I?' I say and put the kettle on.

'There's a letter for you,' says Esme. She holds up a cream envelope and makes a face. 'Hand delivered, and a fancy one too.'

'Weird. Thanks.' I pull a face, put the envelope in a drawer and make the tea.

Later in the morning Esme is busy with a client and when I am satisfied she's concentrating on inking the design I go into the office and pull the letter from the desk drawer. It's got my full name and address written in spiky black fountain pen on a thick cream envelope, but there is no stamp. I open it and pull out a single handwritten sheet on matching watermarked paper; a piece of newsprint flutters to the floor.

24 September 2013

Dear Julia,

I have enclosed something that might jog your memory after our conversation last night. I will be staying at the Holiday Inn in Bradford until Thursday so once you have read the article you can reach me there; there are some matters that I would like to discuss.

I think you owe me an apology for yesterday; you must appreciate I need some answers about my brother and I know that you and Billy were the ones who reported him missing. I have taken the liberty of engaging a private investigator who has furnished me with your addresses at both home and work. I have however been unable to trace Billy's brother so if you could be kind enough to ask him to contact me I would be very grateful.

I would rather you didn't involve the police; they have proved themselves less than competent so far, as you will see from the enclosed cutting.

Yours,

Dr Martin Baxter

I pick up the piece of newspaper from where it has fallen under the desk, unfold it and start to read.

The Guardian

21 August 2013

First Person: The Agony and Uncertainty

Dr Martin Baxter knows he's not the only person to have a close relative go missing, but the circumstances of his brother's disappearance two decades ago were made all the more shocking by the way the police handled the case. As told to Asfia Ali.

"My younger brother Rudy disappeared almost twenty years ago, when he was in his second year of studying engineering at Bradford University. It took several weeks for the full story to come out: although Rudy was reported missing within a few days, his case was never taken seriously, despite the fact he had no reason to disappear: he had no money worries or personal problems. We think he was last seen by his flatmate – who can't be named for legal reasons – on a Saturday night and a week later he still hadn't returned.

A friend of the flatmate informed the university that Rudy had apparently vanished, but no further action was taken until my mother realised that he hadn't contacted her for almost two weeks.

I was in my final year at medical school at the time and I remember mum calling me to say that they were worried because Rudy hadn't been in touch and how she knew that something was wrong. I knew straight away that something bad had happened; the lack of contact was very much out of character. I couldn't trace Rudy either – he didn't answer his phone and there was no reply when I visited him – and that weekend we reported him missing to the police. That was the hardest thing I've ever done.

West Yorkshire police suggested that we hold a press conference in the hope of finding witnesses who might have seen him, but there was a cover-up immediately afterwards which was completely disgraceful.

They suggested there was evidence that Rudy was dealing drugs and that was the reason for his disappearance. There was no further action taken after that; we were told there were no new leads from the press conference and the investigation was quickly shut down. Rudy became a statistic: one more name on the list of the thousands of people who go missing in Britain every year.

That Christmas was very difficult as I'm sure you can appreciate: waiting for Rudy to turn up, wanting him to walk through the door as if everything was fine.

We felt so let down, all of us. You're brought up to trust the police and have faith in them in these situations, but to be told lies like this, by a police force who were more concerned about hiding their own failings by trying to smear Rudy as a drug dealer rather than admit their mistakes: it's completely unfathomable.

Rudy has never been found and there have been no confirmed sightings of him since that weekend. Despite great support from our local MP, who pressed for an inquiry into the catalogue of failings in Rudy's case, we have got nowhere. The police refuse to acknowledge any wrongdoing, and the files concerning his disappearance were alleged to have been lost, which means there are no witness statements or original evidence that could help us. The police have told us that if they re-open the case, this lack of original material will hamper any further investigations.

In 2001 we were encouraged to have Rudy declared legally dead; however this would have enabled the police to close the missing person's file so we declined.

Our mum passed away in the spring and I owe it to her to find out the truth of what happened. She had suffered from agoraphobia since Rudy disappeared; she wasn't able to leave the house even for a minute because she was worried that if Rudy tried to phone she wouldn't be there for him. I know dad was devastated too but kept his feelings to himself: he's from a different generation and we never talked about it. He'd change the subject whenever I mentioned Rudy's name.

I can't describe the catalogue of emotions that you go through in a situation like this. On the one hand, pragmatically speaking, it's likely that Rudy is dead, but you can't help but wonder whether he will come back; you have to hold onto that hope and keep it alive.

I got married in 2002 and Rudy should have been best man. Standing in the church I couldn't help but think about him – would he be married now with a family of his own?

Someone going missing in circumstances such as this leaves a void, a chronic wound that doesn't heal, and above everything else I'm angry that Rudy's life is worth nothing to the authorities.

We are holding a candle-lit vigil in Bradford on the 21st of next month to mark what would have been Rudy's 40th birthday. We hope the vigil will serve two functions: firstly to jog people's memories about Rudy's disappearance in the hope that someone will come forward with new information, but also to raise awareness of all of those missing people who have been let down by the police, whether through negligence or institutionalised failings.

Dr Martin Baxter is a London-based GP. His book "Rudy: A Quest for Justice" is published by Ebury Press and is available in all good bookshops and online retailers.

I put the letter and the newspaper article back in the desk and decide that Martin Baxter is deluded. I have no intention of going to see him and it is some scant comfort that doesn't want the police involved either – albeit for very different reasons to me.

When Esme goes out for a lunchtime sandwich I fasten the Chubb before she is out of sight and search online to find the number for Lynfield Mount. I dial the number with shaky hands; it rings and rings and a receptionist answers when I'm about to hang up.

'Oh, hello. Um...do you have a patient there called Billy Sullivan?'

I can hear her tapping at a keyboard.

'We do.' She asks my name and relationship to Billy.

'Sister-in-law,' I say without thinking.

She rattles off his date of birth; it sounds familiar and I agree that it's the right Billy. I ask about visiting hours and she tells me it's two until six on weekdays; I thank her and hang up.

Chapter Twenty

September 2013

I check the studio diary and find that we've got no clients booked between three and half past four. It feels like some sort of omen, so I suppose I'd better go and visit Billy.

When I get in the car something stops me from putting the key in the ignition and I get out and walk halfway round the block before I persuade myself I'm being stupid, that I really ought to go. I make myself turn around and when I'm finally sitting in the car again I start the engine and switch on the radio as a distraction, but my hands are clenched on the steering wheel and my shoulders are so tense they are almost touching my ears.

On the journey to the hospital I twice think about turning back; it feels as if something is physically pushing me away but I can't explain why I'm so anxious. When I get to the car park I wonder again what I'm doing, and what I hope to achieve by seeing Billy.

I walk through the entrance hoping there might be a queue at Reception, meaning I could turn around and leave before seeing him. I'm ashamed at my cowardice. There is a young man at the front desk and I wait, fidgeting from foot to foot, whilst he finishes his phone call.

'I've come to visit Billy Sullivan,' I say. 'I'm his sister-in-law...' The lie sticks on my tongue this time. 'I was in the area and thought I'd come and say hello.'

He pulls a face and taps something on a keyboard. 'Do you have some form of identification?'

I hand over my driving licence; he checks it and types my details into his computer. Then he phones the ward and tells them that I'm here to see Billy; he asks me to wait and says that somebody will be along shortly to collect me. I sit on a plastic chair and stare at the posters on the wall – a hand-washing reminder, an advertisement for a charity jumble sale – without taking any of it in. I still feel nervous, as if I'm waiting to be called for a job interview.

Five minutes later a nurse appears. 'Julia? Hello, I'm Pat,' she says.

She buzzes us through the security doors to the ward. 'Have you been to see Billy before?'

'Yes,' I stammer. 'Not for a little while though...I've been away.'

'Come with me,' she says. 'Can we have a chat in the office first?'

'Sure.'

She escorts me to a side room and gestures for me to sit down.

'Sorry about this but we're screening all Billy's visitors; your name wasn't on the list at reception. Someone came to see him a day or two ago and there was a problem.'

'How do you mean?'

'Someone we hadn't seen before. He was a tall man, very smartly dressed. He tried to visit Billy.'

I shudder. *Martin Baxter.*

'Go on, what happened?'

'The man came to reception. He knew Billy's name and details although no-one remembered seeing him before so we challenged him for identification and he became very aggressive. He shouted at the receptionist, and threatened one of the nurses.'

'And then...?'

'Security made him leave.'

'Oh my God.'

'Do you know who he could have been?' As you know, with Billy being non-verbal he can't tell us.'

'Non-verbal? Oh – I see. No, I've no idea, sorry.'

'Sister says all visitors have to be registered from now on,' she said. 'We mustn't have Billy upset.'

'Of course not. Thank you, I appreciate it.'

'No problem. Follow me and I'll show you through.'

There are a dozen or so men in the day room and the blinds are half-closed against the low afternoon sun. It smells of school dinners and cleaning products. The television is on, showing an Australian soap opera: a tanned teenage couple argue on the beach with the sound turned off. A half-finished jigsaw lies abandoned on a table. A man – in his fifties, probably, although it's hard to tell from his vacant expression and bloated, stubbled face – sits at the table and mutters at something only he can see. I try not to stare as I scan the room for someone younger with ginger hair and freckles.

'Billy love,' says Pat. 'You've got a visitor. Julia's here to see you.'

This old man in cheap leisurewear can't be him, surely? I stare at him, trying to find a shred of the old Billy but he's unrecognisable: he's put on an enormous amount of weight and his eyes are filmy and dull in his doughy face. His thinning hair is almost colourless and cropped close to his skull. He could be anybody.

'Hi Billy, it's Julia. How are you?'

It's a stupid question, but I have to say something. He looks at Pat warily and makes a noise I can't understand.

She bustles off and leaves us alone; Billy slumps in his chair and won't look at me. He stares at the ground and so I talk about banal things instead – the weather, my day at work – but he makes no sign of acknowledgement. I get the feeling that if he doesn't look at me then it means I'm not really here.

'So, has Sullivan been to see you lately?'

Billy looks at the floor and makes another strange sound that I can't comprehend.

'I'm sorry, what was that?'

There is a painful pause where I can't think of anything to say and Billy continues to softly hoot to himself. I'm sure he's trying to tell me something but I'm frustrated that I can't work out what it might be.

'Well, I – err, I suppose I'd be getting back to work. It's nice to see you again, maybe I should come back when you're feeling a bit more...you know...'

Oily perspiration runs down the back of my neck as I pick up my bag, ready to leave. As I stand up I see a woman in a police uniform walking up the ward; my stomach sinks and guilt washes over me. Maybe she's here about the incident with Rudy's brother: at the thought of Martin I grab onto a chair with clammy hands, afraid that I'll collapse again. Maybe she's here to see me...

'Hello.'

'Afternoon.'

She gives me a perfunctory nod and turns to Billy and says hello. He looks at her and something in his change of expression tells me he knows her; that she's been to see him before. The world moves in slow motion as I try to work out why she's talking to Billy like she's an old friend.

She sits down, takes her hat off and rests it on her lap. She's a petite blonde of about thirty-five and there's something familiar about her: I wonder at first if she's a client from the studio but after a moment the realisation hits me with a rush so hard it physically hurts.

'*Tina*?'

My head is spinning and I can't quite make sense of the fact that it's Tina sitting here and wearing a police uniform. I linger awkwardly with one hand on the back of the chair; I can't decide whether to sit down again or make my excuses and go.

'I'm sorry?' she says. 'Have we met?' She searches my face and I feel as if I'm being interrogated.

I sit down on the hard chair with a thump.

'Yes – we did. It was a long time ago...'

'Really? Did we?'

I run my tongue over dry lips. 'Me and my boyfriend – my ex-boyfriend I mean – he's Billy's brother, we came to stay at the old house in Balldon one weekend. Do you remember?'

'Mmm, vaguely, yes.'

'But you're police now, I can't believe it. I thought you were...'

'You thought I was what?'

'Nothing.'

Tina gives me a professional smile that doesn't quite reach her eyes. 'It's a funny little world sometimes, isn't it?'

I mumble something in reply and make my escape.

I arrive back at the studio just in time for the next client's consultation and I'm grateful for the distraction; seeing Billy in that condition was bad enough but meeting Tina was too strange for words. It feels as if the world has been turned on its head.

The client and I are choosing designs when the phone rings.

'I'll get it,' says Esme from the office. She runs to the reception desk and picks up the ivory princess handset.

'Hello, Yellow Room, how can I help?'

'Hello? Hello?' Esme looks puzzled and puts the phone down.

'Was it a wrong number?'

'No, there was nobody there. Well, *someone* was there because I could hear them breathing, but then they hung up.'

The silent calls happen again half a dozen times. I know who it is and avoid the phone.

'Leave it, the voicemail will get it,' I say to Esme.

'What's going on?' she asks. 'Some strange guy turns up yesterday, and now he's making dodgy phone calls. He's completely unhinged. I don't know who he is Ju, but if you need anything – any time?'

'It'll be OK.' I feel a spasm of self-reproach for the lies I'm telling; I can feel my face go red so I scuttle off to the toilet before she can ask any more questions.

The next time the phone rings Esme is in the office answering emails and the sound of it makes me so angry I ignore my own advice. I pick up the handset and pause for a moment to check it's not a genuine call. Silence echoes at the end of the line and there is the faintest trace of background noise (muffled conversation and the sound of a keyboard: a hotel lobby perhaps, or maybe an office) but nothing identifiable. I keep my voice low and even, so Esme can't hear what I'm about to say.

'Hello Martin. The police have put a trace on the line and we know it's you. Now fuck off.'

There is an abrupt intake of breath and the caller hangs up.

The silent calls stop then, although I linger in the studio until Esme is finished with her admin and we lock up and leave together. When I get home I drive up and down my street, searching for the blue car, but it's gone.

The next day I'm the first one at work and I lock the door from the inside as soon as I get in. When Esme arrives she draws a pen-and-ink sketch of an elegant jade dragon apologising for the security measures and asking customers to ring the bell. We name her Millicent and tape the picture to the glass in the front door.

Whilst we wait for our midday client, I take the laptop into the back room and search for Martin Baxter online. It's a common name and there are hundreds of thousands of results, until I remember the newspaper cutting in the desk.

Searching for the title of his book gives me six hits: one to the original Guardian article, others to the book on Amazon (there are forty-three reviews; it averages four stars) and the final link is to a report in a London local newspaper. I hold my breath and click.

Enfield Independent

6 June 2013

GP Suspended Following Drugs Charge

A family doctor who was found guilty of forging prescriptions for Viagra has been suspended, according to reports.

Dr Martin Baxter, who practised at the Southbury Surgery in Enfield, faced one count of misconduct and was suspended from the GMC register for twelve months following a hearing last Tuesday. He had worked at the Enfield Town practice since 2000.

Giving evidence, Dr Baxter admitted his conduct was inappropriate but stated that it was a "one-off stupid mistake" and that he was suffering from depression at the time but was too embarrassed to seek help for his problems.

No-one from the practice was available for comment.

I can't help but laugh at how ridiculous it sounds and I almost feel sorry for him.

As the morning passes something convinces me the shop is being watched and several times I discreetly check the street when Esme is occupied with other things. By half past twelve Martin's car is back, defiantly parked on the double yellow lines outside Mo's Fried Chicken shop opposite.

'Have you seen the blue Mercedes that's outside?'

Esme pulls a face. 'No, don't think so, you don't get many Mercs round here. Is it Mr Green Man again?'

'Yeah, think so.'

'What's he doing?'

'Nothing. He's just parked outside, watching us.'

'Do you want me to have a word with him?'

'No – but thanks. He'll get bored eventually.'

Esme comes to the window and stands next to me. 'I really fancy a takeaway,' she says, gazing out the window at Mo's shop.

'That sounds marvellous.' I gesture towards Martin's car. 'I'll come with you.'

'It's alright, I'll be fine. What can I get you?'

'Chicken and chips, please. Are you sure you don't want a hand?'

Esme gets her coat and purse from the back room. 'Don't worry; it's only over the road.'

She heads out into the street and walks past the Mercedes without a glance. Martin doesn't move; he's sitting in the car with the engine switched off, watching and waiting.

Ten minutes later she comes back, holding two paper parcels.

'Thanks.' I realise I've been holding my breath.

I make some tea whilst Esme rummages in the kitchenette for a pair of plates. We sit at the reception desk and eat the hot food out of the wrappers, our fingers sticky with salt and grease.

As we finish eating Mo comes out of his shop in his oil-spattered chef's whites, raps on the Merc's window and tells Martin to move his car. Martin says something in reply that makes Mo bang the car's roof with his fist and curse. The commotion makes us both go to the window for a better look.

'Good riddance,' says Esme as we watch the car drive away.

'What did you say to him?'

'Nothing.' She fetches a can of air freshener from under the sink and sprays it around the studio, until the smell of fried food is masked by vanilla and jasmine.

PART THREE

Chapter Twenty-One

15 October 2013

By six o'clock I'm sitting at the laptop with the radio playing in the background and a fresh mug of coffee steaming at my side. I check my diary and see that Esme has booked a couple of hours off this morning to go to the dentist, meaning I'll be on my own for our eleven o'clock client. I think momentarily about calling in sick and asking her to cancel her appointment but that's unfair of me. I'll have to manage.

I open the browser and search for Sydenham Poyntz. My fingers fumble over the keys; at some point in the past twenty years I've forgotten how to spell their name. I click through the band's website to the photos: a few sepia-filtered portraits with Sullivan half in shadow, and a wistful expression on his face as he stares into the middle distance. A wannabe Kurt Cobain is standing next to him, cradling a white Gibson bass as if it were a lover. The next photo is a close-up of a battered drum kit in stark black and white, its owner nowhere to be seen. When I browse through the pictures of Sullivan again I feel tightness in my chest and a strange emotion I can't name.

I click on a couple of the links, searching for contact details: some way of reaching Sullivan to tell him about Rudy. Instead I find a band biography with a link to an obituary for Simon and a list of dates from their most recent tour: half a dozen gigs in places like Scunthorpe and Lancaster in venues with pub names; over three years out of date and nowhere local, nowhere that I recognise.

As I look through the website an avalanche of memories comes crashing down like a flashback: the hours spent travelling to gigs, squashed in the back of Simon's Transit or driving the Wreck; loading and unloading the drum kit; endless games of pool in strange pubs to pass the time; Simon and Sullivan jamming together in our front room for hours at a time as if they could read each other's minds. Rob throwing up in the gutter outside a takeaway after too many lagers, the rest of us laughing and flicking cold chips at him as he retched and swore.

Memories of Billy, too, before he got sick: how at fifteen he thought it was the best thing in the world to come and visit us and be allowed to unload Sullivan's precious guitars into whichever pub the band was playing that weekend, his tongue sticking out the corner of his mouth with the effort of carrying the amp. Sullivan showing his awestruck brother a few basic chord shapes; Jason teaching Billy how to tune a guitar, saying how he was a natural.

I blink hard to get rid of the memories and I search the web again. Sullivan has a personal page on Facebook: his first name is listed as Jeremy and his hometown is Bradford. He has four hundred and six friends and a profile picture that, like the others, must be a dozen years old.

It takes me an hour to write three sentences and when I finally send the message I feel sick and weak. I creep back to bed and try to sleep but it's no use: my mind is racing with frenetic thoughts of Rudy and Sullivan. I toss and turn under the duvet, long-forgotten memories flickering through my mind. I can't believe I've contacted him and I wonder whether I've done the right thing.

I call Esme to let her know I'll be late and I arrive at work barely in time for our client's appointment. The lack of sleep and too much coffee this morning has made me feel paranoid and jittery; all I can think about is the message waiting in Sullivan's inbox.

I covertly check my phone for messages throughout the consultation under the guise of making coffee and unnecessary searches in the back room for folders of designs, but there is nothing. I feel like a teenager again – and not in a good way – until I give myself a talking to about the sad irony of still waiting for Sullivan to call me, twenty years on.

When Esme gets in I manage to leave it for half an hour without picking my phone up but in the afternoon she catches me looking at it for the umpteenth time.

'Are you expecting a call?'

'Sort of.'

She grins. 'Is it a fella?'

I pull a face.

'I knew it!'

'No, no it's not like that. He's an old friend – well, an ex. It's complicated...'

'Oh, this gets better,' says Esme with a grin. She sits down. 'Come on then, tell me all about him. Is he cute?'

I'm not sure who's more surprised when I break down in tears.

'Oh God, Ju, I'm sorry, I was only joking – I didn't mean...'

I blow my nose. 'No, I'm sorry, it's fine, I'm just...' I take a deep breath and start again.

'It's not like that; he's an ex from when I was at university. He was the love of my life – you know how it is when you're young – but we split up. Some really bad things happened and afterwards everything went wrong between us; then his brother got ill and it...it fell apart. Now something's come up – like I said, it's complicated, right – and I've had to contact him again. I'm waiting for him to call, which is why I'm acting like a lovesick teenager.'

'Oh. So what's he called?'

'It's not important.'

'Come on Ju, you know you can tell me.'

'Thanks, but you won't believe it.'

'Try me.'

Fortunately we're not busy because I end up telling her all about Sullivan, from when we met at university through to the way he dumped me, about Billy's collapse into madness, my abortion and Rudy's disappearance – making it sound as if he simply went missing. We're both crying by the time I finish.

'Oh my God, I can't believe you never told me all that before. I didn't realise – I used to love that band. Whatever happened to them?'

I sniff. 'It's not your fault. He was ancient history by the time I opened this place.'

'What are you going to do if he doesn't call you back?'

'I can't do anything; if he doesn't want to reply then I'll have to leave it.'

'But what about Rudy? You said he vanished into thin air – do you reckon he's the one they've found on the moors?'

I feel as if I've been electrocuted. 'How...how do you know about that?'

'It was on the local news on the telly last night. Didn't you see it?'

'No?' My mind is spinning: if it was on the news the police must know who it is – could they tell how he'd died?

'Have a look online, Ju. It's all anyone can talk about.'

'Oh.'

'And don't worry about our five o'clock, I'll do her. You look done in; go home.'

I'm so disturbed by what Esme has told me I'm barely safe to drive across town. When I get home Marwood lets out an indignant chirrup at being woken from his afternoon nap. I make some more coffee although it's the last thing I need, and I sit down in front of the computer, afraid of what I'm going to find.

I look at the *Telegraph & Argus* website and Esme is right. A photograph alongside the article makes it look as if half of West Yorkshire police are searching Baildon Moor and the story tells me that so far they have found the jaw and one or two other bones. It's made the national press as well and the BBC News website has links to some local stories of missing people – a runaway teenager, a young man who vanished after a night out – but they are more recent cases than Rudy's.

I rub my eyes and I wonder for a minute if everyone else has forgotten about him – after all, it was a long time ago – but surely Martin will come forward even if there is the slightest chance of the bones being Rudy's? My body floods with adrenaline and makes my breath come in wheezing gasps; I feel trapped and claustrophobic.

My phone beeps; it's loud in the in the afternoon quiet of the house and it makes me jump. I fumble in my bag and stumble over the security code. It's a text message from an unknown number and part of me hopes that it's junk, something about mis-sold insurance, but another part is desperate for it to be Sullivan: he's the only person who will understand what I'm going through and I've told Esme too much already.

She must think I've completely lost the plot, telling her that I used to go out with Sullivan from Sydenham Poyntz. I wouldn't blame her for not believing a word of what I've said.

I take a deep breath and read the message.

J is that you?

I text back with shaking fingers.

Sullivan? Yes it's Julia.

R has turned up???

Yes. Need to talk to you urgently – please. Are you in Bradford?

After ten minutes' silence I convince myself that he's not going to respond: maybe he's moved away, or he doesn't care, but finally he replies.

Yes. Tomorrow?

Yellow Room studio on Thursby Street – 7.30?

OK.

I take a bottle of red wine from the rack in the kitchen and pour a large glassful, past caring that it's the middle of the afternoon.

Chapter Twenty-Two

October 2013

I spend the next day unable to concentrate: my only thoughts are of seeing Sullivan. The day dawdles by on leaden feet and I'm so impatient I find myself nearly snapping at a client who can't choose between a snake and a cherry blossom design. I send Esme home on the dot of half past five.

I go home, feed Marwood, shower and change – after a few moments of indecision I settle on a grey woollen dress and leggings – and I arrive back at the Yellow Room by quarter past seven. On the way I mentally rehearse what I'm going to say but I have no idea how the meeting is going to pan out. Will he be angry? Pleased to see me?

There is a minicab parked on the corner of the street. As I unlock the door the driver gets out and I wonder if he's made a mistake with the address, but then I see that it's Sullivan.

'Hi.' I can't help but stare at him.

'Julia. Hi.'

The sound of his voice suddenly makes me want to grin but do my best to fight the urge. 'Come in, then.'

He perches on the couch, trying to look relaxed but his eyes dart about the studio and his left knee quivers: he's as nervous as I am. He looks tired and old, like somebody's father, and the bright studio lights do him no favours either. A network of broken veins maps his face, his hair is short and grey and a beer belly strains at his black shirt. I'm shocked at the way he looks; in real life he's far removed from both the Photoshopped pictures on the website and the person that I used to know. The rehearsed conversations in my head dry up and I can't think what to say.

'Would you like some coffee?'

He scratches his neck and clears his throat. 'Have you got anything stronger?'

I take out the emergency bottle of Southern Comfort that we keep under the counter for nervous clients.

'No ice, I'm afraid,' I say and pour an inch into a plastic beaker.

We look at each other for a tense few seconds and both start speaking at the same time.

'How are you?'

'Long time no see.'

My nerves make me giggle. I chew my lip and start again, hating myself.

'You're probably wondering why I got in touch.'

'You said they've found Rudy?' He swallows his drink in one gulp.

'It's been on the news; haven't you heard? Someone out walking his dog found a human jaw and now the police are searching the moor for the rest of him. They've found some other bones by the old mine, you know, where we...'

He puts the plastic cup on the floor. 'It can't be him. No-one would find him down there.'

'You said it was the holding tank. I remember thinking it wasn't very deep.'

He shrugs.

I pace across the studio and clench my fists. 'I thought you knew what you were doing!'

'Why should I have done? You're the one who went crazy.'

'He attacked me! I didn't mean to kill him! But then you took over – you told me what to do, where to go! I trusted you!'

'I was trying to protect us all: Billy, you, me...it was the only place that I knew.'

'I was relying on you!'

Sullivan picks up the plastic cup again and crushes it when he realises it's empty.

He looks away. 'I was frightened too, as much as you and Billy, except the two of you were so wrapped up in yourselves you couldn't see it. I couldn't talk to either of you, I couldn't sleep.'

'I still get nightmares.' I pause. 'Another drink?'

'I shouldn't. I'm working tonight.'

'You drive a taxi these days?'

He shrugs. 'Yeah, kind of, it's just a temporary thing whilst we get the next few gigs lined up.'

'Oh, I see.'

I put the bottle back in the cupboard. Sullivan pulls a tobacco tin from his pocket and starts to roll a cigarette.

'You can't, not in here.'

'I know. Relax.'

'How's Billy? Have you seen him lately?'

He concentrates on making the roll-up and won't look me in the eye. 'Yeah, sometimes.'

'Oh?'

'He's still in hospital. I don't think he recognises me; all he does is sit there staring into space. He doesn't talk, either: sometimes he'll say odd words and that, but it's impossible to have any sort of conversation with him.'

'I'm sorry. It must be hard for you.'

'Yeah. Thanks.'

'What about your mum?'

'Yeah, she's fine.'

'And you?'

'Yeah, fine.'

'I'm sorry to hear about Simon. I know you two were close.'

'Not really, I hadn't spoken to him in years, only through solicitors. He was off his head all the time: dope, crack, even heroin towards the end. He was a total mess. He walked out of a tour and left us right in the shit; it finished the band. We could have really been something, you know?'

'Oh. I'm sorry.'

'Yeah, well. It was a long time ago, there's no point dwelling on it. We are where we are.'

'Fair enough. Look, I need to talk to you. What are we going to do about Rudy? Should we go to the police and say we think it might be him? This is killing me; I don't know what to do...' I'm angry and frustrated and want to cry, but I can't let the tears come in front of Sullivan.

He shifts in his seat. 'You'll be fine. No-one else knows, do they?'

'No. Have you ever told anyone?'

'No. Never.' He puts the roll-up to one side and starts to make another.

'What about Tina? She must have heard something; I screamed the house down.'

'She would have said by now, surely?'

'Do you know where she is?'

'Should I? She's probably a single mum with five kids and living on a council estate.'

'Maybe. Has anyone else spoken to you?'

'No. Like who?'

'Martin Baxter – that's Rudy's brother, right – he's lost the plot, he's written a book all about how the police falsely framed Rudy as a dealer, which of course is a load of rubbish. He turned up here a few weeks ago, I think he went…'

'Fucking hell, no, I never knew there was a brother.'

'Oh yes. He was interviewed on the news when they did the appeal.'

'Appeal? It made the news? Jesus, I never realised. Was that recently?'

'No, it was a few weeks afterwards. Christmas time.'

'I didn't know.'

'And you didn't get a visit from someone who I think was Rudy's dealer? An evil-looking guy with tattoos and a gold tooth?'

'No.' Sullivan shakes his head.

'He turned up here not long after Billy went to hospital. That money Billy took – it belonged to him.'

'Shit. What happened?'

'It was years ago, when this was still Gary's place. He threatened me but he never came back. I don't know what happened to him.'

'No, I never saw him.'

'Lucky you.'

'What will you do? Are you going to wait for the police to show up?'

'I don't know,' I say.

'You won't tell them the truth, will you?' There is a note of pleading in his voice and it jars.

'No. I wish I could have done but I can't. Not now, it's too late.'

He puts one cigarette behind his ear and puts the other in the tobacco tin. He closes the lid and puts it in his back pocket.

'So that's it. Go to the police; tell them you think it's Rudy that the bloke and his dog found. You and Billy were the ones who reported him missing, weren't you? They'll put two and two together and everything will be OK: why would we report him missing if we had something to do with it? Anyway, it's probably not even him.'

'Not him! How many bodies do you think there are out there? You want me to go to the police? You're mad; they'll work out that you were part of it too...we'll both go to prison if the truth comes out. What if there's some new evidence that links us with him – DNA or something?'

'Look, I know you're upset but calm down for a minute, yeah? If you need to go to the police, then do it, but keep me out of it. We've stuck to our story so you have to hang on in there; Rudy went missing that weekend and it's as simple as that. They'll never know any different.'

I can't hold the tears back any longer and start to sob.

'Hey.'

'I'm sorry.' I wipe my eyes with my sleeve.

He puts a hand on my shoulder: tentatively at first, but then he holds me in his arms until with a will of effort I manage to stop crying. He looks at me with genuine concern and I feel a flutter of nostalgia. I hug him back and bury my face against his chest. I can't remember the last time I was this close to a man and it feels strange, but somehow right because it's Sullivan. He smells different to the old Sullivan though: no leather and patchouli now, only tobacco and coal tar soap.

He laughs and ruffles my hair.

'I like it that colour. It suits you.'

'Thanks.'

On impulse I kiss him on the cheek; he's unshaven and his grey stubble is scratchy against my lips. I'm half expecting it when he kisses me back on the mouth; we hug tighter but as I feel his hand run down my thigh I tense and he pulls away.

'Are you going to be OK?'

'I think so, thanks.'

'Look after yourself, yeah?'

'Yeah, you too.'

I watch his back as he leaves and feel a spasm of loss as he drives off. It takes me by surprise and I immediately start to cry again.

Chapter Twenty-Three

October 2013

I slink into work the next morning, tired from another sleepless night; on top of everything else I couldn't stop thinking about Sullivan's kiss and wondering what it meant.

'Morning, Ju.'

I mumble a reply but after my performance two days ago Esme is good enough not to ask me what the matter is. I put the kettle on and whilst it boils I think about what I'm going to do.

I can't see any other option but to take Sullivan's advice and go to the police and tell them that I think they have found Rudy. I try to map out the what-ifs in my head, work out where the conversation might lead, but I can't visualise anything past the point I walk up the steps of the police station.

Maybe I should plan for the worst and put my stuff into storage, ask Esme to look after Marwood, and hand the business over to her. I've got some money put away: not Rudy's, that all went on buying the lease, doing up the studio and getting us through those first few difficult months, but there's enough to keep the business afloat for a while. I suppose I'd have to sell my cottage too, but that would break my heart. Maybe Esme could rent it out? I wonder how long the prison sentence would be for killing Rudy, for hiding his body all these years. Five years? Ten?

I spend all day thinking about it and by closing time the idea of prison is almost worth it to be rid of the guilt. The thought makes me light-headed, almost euphoric, as if a heavy burden has been lifted from my shoulders. I feel like a new woman: I find myself whistling as I put out fresh sharps bins and mentally make lists of everything that I need to get in order before I can go to the police.

'Someone's in a good mood,' says Esme.

'I'm thinking about taking a gap year.'

Esme stops wiping down the chair and looks at me, puzzled. 'Oh. Why's that?'

She must think I've completely lost it. 'I need a break. Everything that's been going on…it's getting me down.'

'Crikey, where did that come from? You're right, though,' she says. 'You're exhausted; you haven't had a holiday in years.'

'But what about Marwood? I can't leave him behind.'

'He's such a honey; I'd love to look after him – if you don't mind, that is?'

'Oh, you're a star; I'll give you the money for his food and the vet and everything.'

'Don't be silly. What about the house?'

'I'll rent the cottage out, put everything else in storage.'

'And this place? You're not thinking of selling, are you?'

'Good God, no. How do you feel about being in charge?'

She grins and it's the only answer I need. 'Where are you thinking of going?'

'I always wanted to see New Zealand.'

It's the first place that comes into my head. I don't even own a passport.

On the way home I feel sentimental and take a detour through West Bowling to look at our old home. The road is exactly the same – bare cobbles and yellow sandstone houses – but when I get out of the car and peer through the railings to the basement the front room is all Ikea furniture and fluffy white rugs; framed black and white photographs hang on walls painted the colour of ripe peaches. It's unrecognisable.

I buy a copy of the *Telegraph & Argus* from the corner shop. The discovery of the body is still front-page news and the article is captioned with a picture of a police officer in white overalls searching the moor.

Bradford Telegraph & Argus

17 October 2013

Baildon Moor Body: More Human Remains Found

Following the recent discovery of human remains by a dog-walker on Baildon Moor, police combing the area surrounding Windy Hill and Low Plain have confirmed the discovery of further body parts.

A spokesman for West Yorkshire Police said, "Further discoveries at the investigation site include a human skull, a fractured thighbone and three vertebrae, all of which were located

> in an abandoned open-cast mine working near the Bingley Road. We cannot comment at this stage whether the discovery is suspicious.
>
> "Members of the public with any information relating to this discovery are asked to contact the incident room by calling West Yorkshire police on 101."

I think the broken leg must have happened when we dropped Rudy down into the holding tank: I don't think I kicked him hard enough to break any bones. I always presumed that I dislocated his knee, but my recall of that night is understandably less than perfect. I think for a moment about asking Sullivan if he remembers but I push the thought away; I'm too embarrassed to call him and I have an inkling of what might happen if we met again so soon. I expect Martin will turn up again any day, though.

It's lunchtime and the Yellow Room is quiet: Esme has gone to the bank and I'm updating the studio Facebook page with photos of some of our recent work. The radio burbles in the background.

The doorbell rings, which strikes me as odd. I'm not expecting anyone until half past one, and these days most women book their appointments over the phone or through our website rather than in person. It's not a client though; when I look through the glass it's the police: a man and a woman, stern and unsmiling in their dark uniforms.

'Hello, how can I help?' My legs are shaking.

'Julia Cox? I'm PC Tom Evans and this is my colleague Sergeant Pozimski,' the male officer says and his colleague nods in acknowledgement. 'We're here to talk to you about a missing person, Rudy Baxter. We believe that you knew him?'

'Mmm.' My jaws start chattering and I suddenly feel light-headed. 'You'd better come in.'

The three of us huddle in the back room. I clear sheets of designs and paperwork onto the far corner of the table, and apologise for the mess and for the fact that there's only two chairs. PC Evans says he will stand and they both refuse my offer of tea. When I sit down my chest is tight and wheezy.

Sergeant Pozimski looks up and I realise who she is.

'Tina?' I blurt and she pauses in the midst of opening her notebook and looks at me. 'We've met before…'

She cuts me off before I can finish. 'I remember,' she says and I wonder what she means, but there's no chance to analyse her reply because they take turns to fire questions at me.

'How did you know Rudy Baxter?'

'When did you report him missing?'

'What was your relationship with Mr Baxter?'

I do my best to answer but I get confused and stumble over dates; I explain how I only met him once, describe how I had to tell the university he'd disappeared because Billy couldn't do it, that he was getting ill even then. I lie that I hadn't thought about Rudy for a long time and how for months I thought he'd turn up one day like nothing was wrong. For good measure I tell them that Billy thought he saw Rudy a few days after he disappeared, and although I know it was a hallucination – a figment of Billy's illness – I leave that out.

'And how often do you see Billy Sullivan?'

'Oh, not often. When I last went to see him it was the first time in years. I can't believe how much Billy's changed...I was shocked, to tell you the truth.'

'What made you go and visit him?'

She knows about Sullivan, about the texts, his visit...did Sullivan go to the police after I saw him yesterday? He wouldn't do that to me, would he? My mouth dries up and I feel as if I'm falling into space.

'Oh, I...I just got to thinking about him, and it made me feel guilty.'

'Why were you feeling guilty?'

'I was ashamed that I hadn't been to see him in such a long time, that's all. We all used to be so close...'

'Hiya!' calls Esme from the front door and I feel weak with relief.

'Hi!' I reply. 'In here.' It's a struggle to keep my voice calm.

She walks in the room, looking pink and windswept. She pulls off her coat and scarf but stops midway through when she sees the two police officers with me.

'Oh my God, Ju, what's happened?'

'Everything's fine,' I say and look at Tina but her face gives nothing away.

'Can I help?' Esme asks.

'It's a personal matter, Miss...?

'Esme – Esmeralda Brennan.'

'Thank you for your time,' says PC Evans. He closes his notebook with a noise like a slap. 'We'll be in touch.'

'Why are you asking about Rudy after all this time? Is it him they've found on the moor?'

They look at each other. 'There have been some new developments in the investigation into his disappearance,' he says.

'Oh. What do you mean?'

'I'm afraid we can't give out information on an active case. Thank you for your time; we'll see ourselves out.'

Tina hands me a business card as they leave. 'Give me a call if you remember anything else, won't you?'

I nod weakly. 'OK.'

'What was that all about?' asks Esme once they've gone.

'Oh, nothing, it was just routine; something about a missing person...'

'It's that man, isn't it?' She fills the kettle and puts a teabag into a mug.

'Yeah, they seem to think so...look, I've got an awful headache coming on. I'm going to take a tablet and sit quietly for a few minutes, OK?

Esme looks at me oddly but makes her tea and then leaves me alone. A panic attack grips me in steely fingers; a flood of nausea and formless terror swallows me up. I sit in the back room, shivering and hardly able to breathe. I can't see properly and my head and heart both feel as if they're about to explode. Blooms of sweat explode across my back and random images flicker through my mind as I sit hunched over the table, feeling like I'm going to die.

After twenty minutes the panic abates to a sort of light vertigo, enough for me to tentatively try to squash it down. I get up warily and brace myself to talk to Esme. In a moment of inspiration I try a Buddhist chant to distract my frantic mind. I silently *om mani padme hum* my way back into the studio to prepare for our next client, but inside I know I can't keep on like this.

For the rest of the day I continue to shake so badly I can barely work – twice I drop something on the floor – although I do my best to hide it.

'What's the matter?' asks Esme.

'Nothing, I just feel a bit funny, I think it's a migraine. I'll be right as rain tomorrow.'

'Come on Ju, this me you're talking to. I can tell a mile off you're not right.'

'I'm fine, honestly. I've been having problems sleeping. I'll be fine.'

'No you're not. Is it to do with that guy?'

'Who?'

'The one who disappeared, what was his name?'

'Who, Rudy? Kind of.'

Esme sits down and looks at me like a worried mother.

'You really need to talk to someone,' she says. 'You look awful; I can tell you're not yourself.'

'I'm not going to the doctor; they'll only give me pills.'

'You've got to do something. I'm worried about you, Ju.'

'I'll be alright. I just need an early night.'

Chapter Twenty-Four

October 2013

I have a feeling of impending doom and as tired as I am, I can't get to sleep. I toss and turn all night and when the DIY superstore opens at seven in the morning I'm already impatiently waiting outside, half deranged with insomnia.

I buy bubble wrap, packing tape and two dozen cardboard storage boxes. On the way home I text Esme to tell her I've been ill during the night, that I'm too sick to come to work. I feel guilty because she will have to cancel a client – but I'm in no fit state to be anywhere near the studio today: I'm still shaking and feel as if I'll be sick any minute.

I spend the rest of the day packing. I wrap precious things up in the bubble wrap and boxes and label them for storage. I throw most of my clothes into bin-bags for someone to take to the charity shop. I pack a small suitcase full of essentials: a change of clothes and clean underwear, my phone charger, some toiletries and my best hairbrush.

I grab a sheet of paper and write a letter to Esme, trying to explain everything to her and make some sort of sense of the past few weeks. The list of things to remember seems endless.

Dear Esme,

If you're reading this then I've been arrested. Don't worry, I'll explain everything in a minute – and I've been expecting this to happen for years so it's not a surprise.

I'm afraid there never was a gap year. All I wanted was to make sure that you would be alright without me and it's the only way I could think of to start the conversation.

But to begin with there are some practical things to sort out: the Yellow Room, Marwood, the cottage, so please bear with me.

Thank you for offering to look after Marwood. There's a bag of his food in the kitchen cupboard – thirty grams twice a day and a third of a can of rabbit Whiskas – it's the only flavour he'll eat. His vet is the one behind the bingo hall.

As for the Yellow Room, I know you'll be fine managing the studio on your own but please take on someone else to help. I've transferred enough money into the bank account to cover any emergencies. The statements and cheque book are all in the studio safe and of course everything's in both our names. There's a direct debit set up for the rent.

Now, the cottage: I don't know if they'll make me sell it (I hope not) but everything is packed away ready so please rent it out, if you're allowed. Stuff labelled in boxes is for putting in storage but everything else can go. I've put a key under the pot of lavender in the front garden and the car keys are on the hook in the kitchen: the car is yours if you want.

As for my being arrested: Esme, I killed someone. That body on Baildon Moor, the guy Rudy who went missing that I told you about? I killed him. It was an accident, but I'm not expecting any sympathy. He attacked me one night after a party when everyone else was asleep. I tried to fight him off and he fell and hit his head on the floor and died. I panicked and put his body in the back of my car and dumped him in the old holding tank on Baildon Moor. I always knew that he'd be found one day.

That's the real reason I've been so stressed. Ever since that man and his dog found the bones on the moor I've known it was only a matter of time before the police would come for me. It's a relief in a way: I've lived with this hanging over me for twenty years, and now Rudy's family will get the answers that they deserve at last.

I'm so sorry Esme, please forgive me.

J. xx

I leave the letter on the kitchen table, weighted down by a tin of cat food and I'm as ready as I ever will be. I pick up Marwood and kiss him goodbye (he purrs and chirrups at me, which makes me cry because I know I won't see him again) and feed him double quantities of food to tide him over until Esme can come round.

When they arrest me I'll use my one phone call to ring her, to let her know what's happened. She's had a spare key to the cottage for years but I've left another one to be on the safe side.

I put the suitcase in the back of the car and drive into town very carefully, staying under the speed limit all the way. It's funny, but I don't feel nervous now. The fog in my head has cleared and I feel calm, even serene. I'm in control at last.

The police station is in an ugly yellow building and a cluster of teenagers lurk outside, furtively smoking. As I park, my heart starts pounding again so I take a deep breath and push my hands into my pockets. I walk up the steps and through the sliding glass doors with my shoulders back and my head held high.

Inside, the station is brightly lit and has the cloying institutional smell of unwashed bodies and cheap disinfectant; the floor is scuffed and worn. There is a long desk behind a thick plastic screen and uniformed staff sit at computers. I force a smile and make eye contact with the friendliest person I can see.

'Um, hi.'

'Can I help you?' she says.

'I'm here about a missing person.'

She looks at me, searching my face; she can see my guilt straight away.

'It's about the body on Baildon Moor. I need to talk to Tina...Sergeant Pozimski...she came to see me the other day...'

Time slows to a crawl as the woman takes me to an interview suite off the foyer. She leaves me to wait and stew for fifteen minutes whilst she searches for Tina. By the time she arrives I've wound myself up into a tight ball of nerves again and my right eye starts to twitch as if it has developed a mind of its own.

Tina sits down opposite me and gives a well-rehearsed explanation of how the interview will be videotaped. I nod and listen, and try to ignore the fact the chairs and table are bolted to the floor.

'I'll need to take some details,' Tina says. She's calm and it only serves to heighten my own dread.

My voice wavers as I give her my name and address and date of birth; she asks how I first knew about the body on Baildon Moor and that throws me. I stammer and tell her it's been all over the newspapers, on the television news.

'And you say you've got information that may assist the enquiry?'

'I...I know it's Rudy Baxter.'

'Tell me why you think that?'

My quivering legs suddenly take on a life of their own and I flee. Some primeval instinct takes over as I run down the corridor and I can't think of anything apart from getting away.

For a frantic second the door won't open until I remember to press the green button on the wall and I escape onto the street, taking the steps two at a time. I can hear Tina calling my name as she follows me down the stairs. I run to the car and fumble for the key.

'Julia! Wait!'

I ignore her, get into the car and bunny-hop out of my parking space. The car shudders and stalls and as I restart the engine I see Tina in the rear-view mirror. She's getting into her own car – something small and silver – and somehow I need to get away from her before she catches up with me. I pull away into the traffic on the main road with no idea where I'm driving to; I can't go home – if my packed belongings aren't suspicious enough the letter to Esme certainly will be – and I can't go to the Yellow Room so I head north at a steady thirty miles an hour, afraid to change lanes or go any faster because I'm hysterical and shaking with absolute, consuming terror. Every gear change is a superhuman effort of co-ordination and self-control.

By the time I reach the river out at Shipley I still have no sense of where I'm heading. I think that I catch the occasional glimpse of Tina's silver car but I can't be sure whether it's really her, or my own paranoia making me think she's still following. There are fat dark clouds on the horizon ahead of me and it's going to start raining any minute.

I'm lost, but these winding roads look familiar and a gut instinct tells me to turn left. I'm all gut instinct now; some animal part of my brain is all that still functions beneath the panic. I turn left and find myself in a high street. There's a café, an estate agents and a chemist's shop, and I think I recognise the weathered sandstone buildings.

I reach a roundabout and take the first turning because I'm unable to cope with anything more complicated. When I'm safely over the junction I park badly in a narrow side lane between a pub and a church, away from the main road and where I can't be seen. I look up at the pub sign and see this is the Bull's Head in Baildon, where we went with Rudy, Billy and Tina all those years ago. A wall of fatigue hits me. I lean over the steering wheel and start to weep from exhaustion.

There is a knock at the driver's side window: it's probably somebody complaining about my parking, I wouldn't be surprised if I'd blocked off the whole street. I wipe my face with my hands and look up, ready to apologise and move.

It's Tina. I slump back over the steering wheel and close my eyes in the hope that she will go away, but she taps at the window again.

'Julia?' She mouths my name through the glass.

'Go away. Leave me alone.'

'Julia, please can I talk to you?'

For a moment I consider starting the car, reversing back down the narrow lane but she'll only follow me again, and anyway, where could I go? I pull the window down and it suddenly starts to rain: cascades of water fall from the flat dull sky.

'Go into the pub. I'll see you there.'

She looks doubtful. 'OK,' she says at last and jogs back to the main road, holding her hat in place with her hand.

I pull my hair off my face and rummage in my bag for a tissue to blow my nose and wipe my eyes. I think again about leaving Tina waiting in the pub whilst I drive home, but I need to go through with this: I can't bottle out now, everything's gone out of control. What if she called back to the station on her way here and her colleagues are waiting for me at the cottage or the studio? I push the idea from my mind and calm my breathing down as much as I can, lock the car and follow Tina into the pub.

She is sitting at a corner table with a glass of water. I walk over to join her and try to smile.

'Hi.'

'Hello Julia, I'm glad you decided to come.'

'I didn't have a choice, did I? Can I get you a drink?'

'I've got one already. Thanks.'

I need something stronger than iced water so I order a vodka and tonic.

As the barmaid makes my drink I look around. The pub has changed – there's no pool table any more, no burbling fruit machines or fug of smoke at the bar: instead the walls are wood-panelled and painted in muted, chalky colours; a blackboard advertises hot drinks and real ales. My hands are still shaking enough that the ice rattles as I put the glass on the table.

I watch the rain lash at the windows and wait for Tina to say something but she doesn't. The silence becomes first awkward and then oppressive.

'I can't believe you followed me.'

She takes a sip of her water. 'I needed to make sure you were alright.'

'Haven't you got to get back to work?' I look at my watch and see that somehow it's half past three. I have a vague sense of time dragging me away on its undertow.

'No. I'd like to have a chat with you.'

'OK.'

'Why did you come here?'

I take a deep swallow of my drink and its icy bitterness helps clear the fog from my head.

'I don't know, I got in the car and drove. I didn't know where I was going, I was really upset...'

'But you've been here before?'

'Not for ages. Years. How do you know?'

'You seemed to know where you were going.'

'Not really. I guess I came here on autopilot – you know sometimes your subconscious takes over…'

'You were thinking about Baildon when you came to the station.'

'Yeah.' There's a fork of lightning and a clap of thunder from the direction of the moor; with my ragged nerves it makes me jump and some of my drink splashes onto the dark polished wood of the table.

'Yes…I was thinking about Rudy because of what's been on the news, in the paper. I keep having these nightmares and I'm so anxious all the time – shaking, I can't concentrate. Esme got really worried because none of this is like me at all, I've been crying at work, not able to sleep, a real mess.'

'I see,' she said.

'You remember me, don't you?'

'Slightly, I think. You said you used to go out with Billy's brother?'

'Sullivan, that's right – we came to stay with Billy one weekend, do you remember? I gave you a lift home to Buttershaw; I had an old Land Rover and pink hair…'

'Yes, it was not long before Billy got ill, wasn't it?'

My heart is starting to race again so I take another gulp of vodka. The alcohol has gone to my head – I've eaten nothing all day – and I feel slightly dizzy, but despite it the earlier panic attack surges back and I feel as if I'm standing outside of my body and staring down at myself. I look past Tina and out through the window; the rainclouds have dispersed as quickly as they came and there is a patch of blue sky far above us.

'Julia – Julia,' she says gently. 'Is there something wrong?'

I drink some more; my glass is three-quarters empty now. 'I…I…' The tears return again and Tina waits for me to pull myself together.

'I'm sorry – it's brought everything back – what happened at Baildon – meeting you again…I'm sorry, it's like I'm having a flashback or something…'

'Would you like to tell me about what happened at Baildon?'

'I don't know where to start.' The words come out high-pitched and thready, it sounds like an old lady's voice.

'Don't worry, and start at the beginning,' she says.

I look around the pub and I'm relieved to see it's still empty except for the two of us; the barmaid is in the other bar where she has her back to us. She is polishing a glass whilst chatting on a mobile phone wedged under her ear.

'It was that weekend when Sullivan and I came to stay with Billy, it was the first time that we'd seen his new house since he'd gone to uni. He invited us over for the weekend, and you had too much to drink and were ill, so I p…put you to bed…' I stammer and look at her, begging her to remember but she shows no sign.

'Then we went to bed; Sullivan and I camped out in the front room. I woke up in the middle of the night, I needed a drink of water and Rudy…Rudy was still up, sitting in the kitchen. He had the telly on…and…and…'

'It's alright, Julia, take as long as you need.'

'He was watching a porn film…I didn't know he was there, if I'd got dressed none of this would have happened, it was all my fault…I went to the sink, turned on the tap and it was so noisy…I didn't hear him…'

I squeeze my eyes shut, reliving those final moments in the kitchen at the farmhouse and I can see everything exactly as it was that night: the tiled floor, the old-fashioned stone sink with the dull grey taps, the great black Aga looming in the corner.

'He grabbed me from behind. He put his hand in my knickers and put his other hand over my face, I couldn't breathe, I thought I was dying. He said something to me – I think it was "I know you want this" – I can't remember his exact words but his voice, I can hear him like it happened yesterday. He licked my face, he smelt sweaty, like meat…'

I open my eyes to bring myself back to the present day, and look at Tina. Straightaway I can tell she's upset: she catches me looking and puts the professional smile back on but it looks broken and doesn't fit her face any more. I must have said something wrong. I'm panicking, nauseous and shaking again from reliving Rudy's attack and now I hate myself for making Tina suffer too.

'Are you alright?'

She nods. 'How did that make you feel?'

'How did I feel? I was terrified, I thought he was going to kill me, rape me...I was scared and I'd never felt so alone. Sullivan was asleep at the other end of the house and Billy was upstairs. Nobody could hear what was going on, I couldn't even scream.'

'What happened next?'

'His hand was still in my knickers. He was, you know, groping me down there…I was still trying to get free. I was going to die. I managed to elbow him in the ribs and he fell down, he banged his head…'

'It's OK, Julia, just take your time and tell me what happened.'

'I screamed and screamed and then Sullivan came in. Rudy was lying on the floor; I thought he'd knocked himself out.

Sullivan checked for a pulse but I was still screaming and then Billy came downstairs.' I swallow the rest of my drink and stare at the wall.

'Please, go on.'

'I can't.'

'I know this is difficult for you. Take a minute if you need to.'

'I can't, I'm sorry.' I push back the chair and stand up. 'I need some air, OK?'

'I'll come with you.'

'No, please – I need to be on my own.'

Tina follows me out anyway. The barmaid is still chatting on the phone, oblivious to our conversation. The sun is shining now and it gives the autumn air a hallucinogenic clarity. There is a rainbow over the moor and I walk towards it: once again I don't know where I'm heading; I'm just trying to get away from all the memories in the pub.

Tina walks with me in silence as I head up a side-street full of new bungalows: rabbit hutches with trim gardens, conservatories, neat driveways. After a few hundred yards the road peters out into a muddy track that leads off towards the open countryside. I follow it and there is a wooden bench set back from the path, with a view over Baildon Moor. I stop and look around and when I realise where we are I laugh out loud.

'Are you alright?' says Tina.

'The farmhouse – it must have been about here...the house where Billy and Rudy lived. Oh my God, it was here! It was here!' I lift my face and hands to the sky and roar with laughter at the insanity of it all.

I pick my way up the path but my boots slip in the greasy mud. I sit on the damp bench and I'm still laughing but it's verging on the hysterical now. Tina sits down next to me.

'Are you sure you're OK?'

I bite the inside of my cheek until the pain makes me wince and the laughter dissolves to hiccups. 'Yeah.'

'Do you want to tell me what happened next?'

I stare at the wide expanse of moor and sky. The rainbow has gone now, replaced by scudding clouds.

'I'm sorry. I can't.' I gesture at her uniform.

'Whatever you tell me, it won't go any further.'

'Really? Can you do that?'

'Absolutely. You have my word.' She takes off her hat and smiles at me but she looks sad and resigned. 'You have to trust me on this one, OK?'

'I took him to Baildon Moor in the back of my car and left him there. I wonder what happened to him.'

'And your boyfriend helped you?'

I shake my head. 'Did Billy tell you that?'

'No, I'm curious.'

'No. Sullivan had nothing to do with it. I did it on my own.'

'I see. Good.'

'Good? Why?'

'Good riddance to him,' she says and looks me straight in the eye.

'*You what*?'

'You weren't the only person he attacked.'

'What? I don't understand?'

She looks me straight in the eye. 'Julia, Rudy assaulted me too.'

The world turns itself inside out and I feel dizzy again. I grip the damp wooden arm of the bench to steady myself.

'You? You too? Oh my God...'

She nods. 'It happened at the house when Billy wasn't around; it got so that I wouldn't be in the same room as Rudy on my own. Once he pushed me against the kitchen wall and kissed me; he grabbed my breasts and told me I was asking for it because I wasn't wearing a bra. If Billy hadn't come in...'

'Oh Tina, I'm so sorry.'

'Thanks.'

'Did Billy ever know what Rudy did to you?'

'No, I never told him. I thought he'd be angry.'

'What about your mum, a teacher, someone like that?'

Tina shakes her head. 'I didn't tell anyone. I rationalised it by convincing myself I deserved it.'

'Oh, you poor thing.'

She sighs. 'One Mum's boyfriends used to be the same. He'd pat me on the backside and tell me I was jailbait, that I'd get some bloke locked up if I wasn't careful, dressing the way I did. I was twelve.'

'Fucking hell, that's awful.'

'So I didn't expect any sympathy from anyone about Rudy. To cut a long story short it's one of the reasons I joined the police: to try and do what I could to stop men like him.'

'Good on you.'

'Let's talk about Rudy again for a moment. You say you left him on the moors?'

I can't look her in the face. 'Yes.'

'Whereabouts?'

'In one of the old mineshafts.'

'Why did you do that?'

'He was dead: he wasn't breathing. I wanted it to look like he'd had an accident; I didn't know what else to do.'

'Why didn't you call the police?'

'They wouldn't have believed what Rudy had done and that it was an accident. I was half undressed, so it was my fault in a way too. Sullivan had a criminal record for assault and we'd been smoking dope all night. The police wouldn't have believed the truth.'

'Is he still there?'

'You know those bones on Baildon Moor? It's him, I know it is.'

'Why do you think that?'

'I don't know, it's a feeling I've got, a part of me always knew that one day someone would find him. That's why I came to see you. I couldn't stand it any longer, knowing that the police would find a connection between us and work out what happened; I nearly died of fright when you came to the studio.'

'Mmm, I could tell.'

'What about your colleague; did he say anything to you after you interviewed me?'

'All he knows is that you were the one who originally reported Rudy missing, and that it was a routine visit. It'll be fine.'

'So the police have found the rest of the bones on the moor – I know it's Rudy – and then you'll arrest me and I'll go to prison.'

'Tell me why you think you'll have to go to prison.'

'I attacked him and dumped his body on the moors, I'm guilty. Sullivan and I are the only people who were there that night, apart from you and Billy of course. They'll realise that we were involved when Rudy disappeared and therefore we must have been the ones that killed him. He didn't deserve what I did to him. End of story.'

'But what if Rudy had gone for a walk on the moors when he was drunk, or high maybe? We know he was a drug dealer. It's a dangerous place, especially at night. Maybe he couldn't see where he was going and fell into one of the open mines.'

'Do you really think it's his body they've found?'

'I can't say too much about it, obviously, but there are one or two other candidates – men of the right age and height who were reported missing in the area. But my personal view is that yes, it's definitely him.'

'Does anyone at work know about your connection with him?'

'No. I should have said something before,' she shrugs. 'It's too late now; I'd get suspended if anyone found out. I'd probably lose my job.'

We sit in silence for a minute, staring at the horizon and letting it all soak in.

'How did you find out about Billy being in the hospital?'

'I thought he'd dumped me to begin with. I didn't hear from him for a week, it was as if he had disappeared off the face of the earth; we normally spoke or saw each other every day. Then he phoned me and said he was staying with you, he said that Rudy had gone missing and he couldn't stay in the house on his own.

He sounded frightened and not himself – but of course, I had no idea what was happening.

'He didn't call me back, and I didn't have your number or address so I bunked off school and went to the house in Baildon. His mother answered the door and said he was ill, that he'd had some sort of breakdown and that he was in the old psychiatric hospital. I went to visit but they wouldn't let me in at first; the nurse said it was family only so I lied and said I was his cousin. He didn't recognise me, he was just...gone.' She makes a small, pathetic gesture.

'Oh Tina, if only I'd had some way of letting you know. I feel so bad.'

'It's OK. I still visit every few weeks.'

'Really? After all this time?'

'I couldn't bear to think that he'd been forgotten and left on his own.'

'I don't think his brother goes to see him very often.'

'What's his take on all this?'

'We split up not long afterwards – he went off with someone else; I think it was partly because of what happened...it drove him away. It was messy, really horrible. I had an abortion too, I hadn't even realised I was pregnant when we broke up. But I spoke to him a little while ago and he told me I should go to the police and tell them that it's Rudy. He knows what I did but it was all down to me; he doesn't know exactly where I put Rudy's body. Billy knew what I'd done too, but afterwards he told himself that Rudy went out one day and simply vanished. I think he actually believed it in the end.'

'Julia,' she says and looks at me again, serious this time. 'Listen to me. What you did was self-defence; Rudy attacked you.

I like to think I would've fought back too, had it been me in your position. If you want my opinion – and this is a personal one, not a professional one – he deserved everything that happened to him.'

'Really? Why do you say that?'

'I've no doubt about it. And that is why I'm not going to repeat what you told me.'

I sag against the hard bench and feel like crying with relief.

'I can't believe you'd lie for me.'

'Sometimes this job is about doing the right thing, not doing things right.'

Chapter Twenty-Five

October 2013

When I get home I'm shattered and have a headache that feels as if someone has cleaved my skull in two. I don't bother unpacking; it would be too much like tempting fate to empty my suitcase and all the boxes and bags, but I burn the letter to Esme and wash the ash down the kitchen sink. Afterwards I lie down on the sofa and fall asleep, but the nightmares come back: I'm locked in the condemned cell again, waiting to be hanged for murder but I wake up at the moment the warders come to take me to the scaffold.

I'm so exhausted I doze off again and sleep through the whole evening; it's dark outside when I wake up. I go up to bed but spend most of the night awake, my conversation with Tina playing over and over in my head. Did I really do the right thing? Is she really going to keep her promise to me? I have a deep craving for some other reassurance that everything is going to be all right, some advice on what I should do next.

I toss and turn in bed until Marwood comes and purrs into my ear. I scratch his neck and we fall asleep together with his paw brushing my shoulder. I'll go and see Maggie tomorrow, I think as I eventually drift off. She'll know what to do.

Maggie's shop is a cavern of velvet and crystals. Glass display cabinets hold a selection of silver gemstone jewellery, dozens of silk scarves are draped on a rack by the door and it all smells of incense and jumble sales.

The shop is empty. 'Hello? Is anyone in?'

'Out here, pet,' Maggie replies.

I find my way to the back of the shop where Maggie is sitting on a folding patio chair. She has a red bandanna knotted over her grey hair and a faded pack of tarot cards is stacked on the table in front of her. A fat brown spaniel snores in front of a Calor gas heater.

She beams. 'Julia! What a lovely surprise. How are you?

'I'm alright, thanks. I...I need some advice...' I stammer. 'I wondered if you could do my cards?'

'Of course I can. Sit down, pet,' she says. 'I'll put the kettle on.'

I make myself comfortable on the canvas chair and whilst Maggie makes us tea I look around. The big Welsh dresser still stands against the back wall, and its shelves are full of well-worn paperbacks – half a dozen Jackie Collins novels and a copy of Jilly Cooper's *Riders* catch my eye. An electronic cigarette lies on the table next to the tarot deck.

When Maggie returns with a tray laden with a teapot, two mugs and a packet of biscuits, I shuffle and cut the deck and pick out four cards. Maggie lays them out on the table: the Queen of Wands, the Page of Swords, the Devil, the Hanged Man. I flinch, thinking of my recurring nightmare of the condemned cell, the faceless black-uniformed prison warders and the noose tight against my throat.

'Oh!' I drop the final card on the table as if it's red-hot.

Maggie picks it up and lines it up with the others. 'The Hanged Man reversed,' she says. 'Interesting.'

'What do you mean? Is it bad news?'

'Don't be afraid: this card is about acceptance and wisdom, not death. Do you see the man is smiling, despite the fact he's hanging upside down from a tree?'

I nod.

'As you know, the most obvious answer to a problem is not always the best one; you need to confront things to gain wisdom. By hanging, the man has achieved a sort of enlightenment because he's seeing the world with new eyes.'

'What does it mean?'

'There's something bothering you, and you need to look at it in a different way.'

'And how do I do that?'

Maggie looks at me quizzically. 'Sometimes you have to give up something you have in exchange for something you want.'

'I don't understand. What do you mean – like a sacrifice?'

'Possibly. But more likely it's an old point of view you need to let go, and get a new perspective on whatever it is. You need a holiday. Take some time out to look at your problems from a distance and everything will make more sense.'

'Oh, OK. I see.'

'You've been working too hard; you've lost perspective and need to look at life from another direction. There's someone who's been holding you back, and you need to let them go.'

I say nothing and nod again.

She picks up another card. 'Were you thinking about travelling?'

'Yes…I was thinking about going to New Zealand.'

Maggie beams. 'Good,' she says. 'You've earned it. But before you go, there's one last piece of unfinished business that you need to sort out.'

I pull a face. 'What's that?'

She taps the Page of Swords. 'A young man,' she says. 'Don't forget about him.'

'Are you sure? I don't know any young men.'

Maggie picks up the card and looks deep into the pattern. 'Maybe he's not as young as he was.'

'No. I don't know.'

'Maybe you haven't been as close to each other as you might have liked.'

I shake my head. 'I'm sorry. I can't think who you mean.'

'It's not me pet, that's the cards you chose telling you that.'

I look at the cards on the table, their orientation and order, the secret symbols hidden in each picture and I sigh. 'Maggie, how do you do all this stuff? What's your secret?'

She laughs her wheezy smoker's laugh. 'Years and years of practice: that and a good dose of common sense.'

I still don't understand, but when I leave I cross her palm with a twenty-pound note.

On the drive home, I get stuck in a traffic jam and whilst I wait for the lights to change, the realisation suddenly hits me: Maggie's cards were telling me to go and see Billy. He's the only person I know who fits the description. How could I have been so wrapped up in myself to not have seen that?

I argue with myself about going back to visit Billy in the hospital. I don't want to – he won't recognise me, that much is certain – and I feel uncomfortable at how much he has changed. But if Maggie says that the cards want me to go and see him then I suppose I'd better do what they tell me.

I drive over at lunchtime and tell myself it won't take long: I'll let him know I'm off travelling, tell him I hope he's being looked after alright, that sort of thing; just a few minutes for me to say goodbye.

A middle-aged man is sitting at the front desk when I arrive. I mention Billy's name and he taps something into his computer.

'Billy Sullivan?' he says. 'He's been transferred to the Infirmary.'

'Transferred? What's the matter?'

'Are you a relative?'

'Sort of.'

He looks at me with something that seems like pity. 'Unless you're a relative I can't give out any information. It's Data Protection, I'm afraid.'

'It's fine. I'll go down there myself.'

I wonder what on earth could have happened to mean that Billy needed to be moved to another hospital. The five-minute drive down the back lane to Bradford Royal Infirmary seems to take much longer.

The receptionist at the front desk of the BRI directs me down a long white corridor to the Cardiac High Dependency Unit and in turn the ward clerk there shows me to a waiting room whilst she finds a member of staff who can tell me what's wrong with Billy.

The unit is eerily quiet and full of patients in blue hospital robes, wired to rhythmically beeping machines. It smells of disinfectant and antiseptic hand gel which is strangely comforting because it reminds me of the studio, although here it is mixed with an undertone of other, less familiar scents.

Sullivan is sitting in the relatives' room. For a moment I'm surprised to see him; for some reason he didn't factor in any of the scenarios I was thinking through on my way here.

He's unshaven and looks crumpled.

'Oh. Hi.'

He grunts. 'What are you doing here?'

'I went to visit Billy and they told me he'd been transferred. What's the matter?'

'He's had a heart attack.'

'Oh my God. Is he going to be alright?'

Sullivan shakes his head and looks as if he's going to cry.

'Oh no, I'm so sorry.' I sit down next to him on the plastic couch and put a hand on his arm.

'I didn't know you visited,' he said.

I feel guilty that I've only seen Billy once. 'Not very often.'

Sullivan looks at his hands and doesn't reply.

'Is your mum on her way?'

He clears his throat. 'Yeah. Naz's driven over to Salford to pick her up.'

'Naz? Is he a friend?'

'Nazneem. She's my wife.'

'Oh.' I think of our embrace in the studio and the conversation ebbs away.

The doctor comes in; he's young but looks tired and defeated, with dark rings under his eyes.

'Mr Sullivan?'

We look at the doctor expectantly and I hope – although I somehow know it is without foundation – that he's going to give us good news and say that Billy is going to be alright. Instead he tells us that Billy has died, that the heart attack was so serious there was nothing they could do to save him.

'Fuck! No!' Sullivan roars and breaks down in tears.

'I'm sorry, I'll come back in a few minutes,' says the doctor and he scuttles away, leaving the two of us alone in the bright white room.

I can't think of the right thing to say. I put my arm around Sullivan in an awkward attempt at a hug. I'm surprised when he reciprocates, and we sit clumsily holding each other as he cries.

'I let him down,' he sobs. 'I should have gone to see him; mum always said I should go more often.'

'Hey...it's OK.' I give him a tissue from my handbag. 'You did what you could to help.'

He blows his nose; he looks so desolate and vulnerable it brings tears to my eyes too. 'No I didn't, and I hardly ever went – that place, it was so *horrible*, you know?'

'I know.'

'I'm sorry,' he says after a long silence.

'What for?'

'I'm sorry for everything: for the way I treated you and Billy, and Simon when he got messed up. I didn't know what I was doing.'

'Hey, come here.' I give him another hug and hold him close to me; he clings to my shoulder and I stroke his hair. 'It's OK, I forgive you. We both did some silly things. We were young and we couldn't deal with it: we were only kids.'

'I let Billy down. I should have been there for him, should have done something when he first got ill but I couldn't cope with it, I ran away...I couldn't face seeing my own brother in that state. I can't forgive myself.'

His phone rings and I watch him fight back tears and struggle to articulate the words to Naz to say that Billy has died; in any other circumstance I would put my arm around him but it seems wrong to do that when he's on the phone to his wife. One half of me is tempted to stay and find out what she's like but another part of me doesn't want to meet her – or see Barbara again, especially at a time like this. The sensible, cowardly part of me wins.

'I'd better be going. Are you going to be OK?'

'Yeah, thanks. They'll be here any minute.' We hug again and I leave without looking back.

On my way out of the unit I see Sullivan's mum and another, much younger woman walking down the corridor towards me. Barbara looks old and frail, faded by grief. They are followed by two boys of about ten and twelve who are arguing. The younger woman wears a harried expression; she tosses her long black hair and shouts at them.

'Dylan! Harrison!' Stop it!'

'But muuuum...!' the eldest pleads. He is the image of Sullivan.

The boys briefly stop squabbling. I give Naz a brief nod of acknowledgment and carry on walking.

As soon as I get back to my car I fish Tina's business card out from where I've hidden it in the back of my purse. I call the mobile phone number and leave a message to let her know what has happened to Billy. I sit in the car park, trying to gather my thoughts and when she phones me back a few minutes later we both cry a little when I tell her that he has died.

I'm surprised when she asks about the funeral but then I realise that she was a better friend to Billy than anyone, even Sullivan. She asks if I want to come with her and I find myself saying yes. She tells me she'll get the details from the hospital and I give her my phone number as if it were the most natural thing in the world.

Chapter Twenty-Six

November 2013

Tina and I meet at the crematorium on a miserable, windy afternoon with a sky like wet concrete. I'm relieved to see that she's dressed in a black trouser suit and not her police uniform, but I suppose that she's here on a personal visit and not a professional one. We watch the hearse arrive and four pallbearers carry the coffin into the crematorium; Tina's eyes well up as they pass but I can't feel anything. In a way death was a release for him. The Billy I knew died years ago.

There are fewer than a dozen people here. Tina and I sit in the back row of the sparsely filled chapel with two nurses from the hospital that she seems to know well; she introduces me to them as a friend of hers.

Sullivan notices us walk in and out of the corner of my eye I see him whisper something to his wife whilst I'm exchanging pleasantries with the nurses; I wonder if he's explaining who we are.

The minister is a bald, lugubrious man with crooked teeth. He knows nothing about Billy and calls him William throughout the short service; I can hardly bear to listen because it makes

Billy sound like someone's grandfather. Tina winces when he says the name.

The references to William George Sullivan and the vicar's generic platitudes mean I drift away and entertain a fantasy that we're somehow all at the wrong funeral, that it's not Billy lying here in the cheap coffin with plastic handles, it's somebody else entirely. Sullivan's children look bored and I wonder how often they visited Billy in hospital. I think I can guess the answer.

After twenty minutes it's all over: we murmur the Lord's Prayer, sing *All Things Bright and Beautiful* and traipse out of the chapel into the grey afternoon.

There's so few of us that it's almost inevitable Tina and I bump into Sullivan and his family outside.

'Hi,'

'Hi.'

'I'm so sorry about Billy.'

'Yeah, thanks.'

We look at each other awkwardly for a few seconds; we've already run out of things to say.

'We're having a small gathering at the house afterwards, if you and your friend would like to come?' says Barbara. 'I'm sorry dear; I didn't catch your names?'

'Thank you, it's very kind of you, but I really must be getting back. I'm Julia, by the way. And this is Tina; you might remember her. She's an old friend of Billy's.'

There is another embarrassing silence. 'I'm sorry,' I say to Sullivan again as we turn to leave.

'Who was that, Jez?' Naz says to our backs.

Tina and I walk to the car park together and I'm lost in my own thoughts, trying to figure out how Sullivan has become Jez the husband, the father, the taxi driver. When I look up I see a dark blue Mercedes parked in the far corner.

'Shit.'

'What's the matter?' says Tina, suddenly professional and alert.

'That car, the navy Merc. That's Martin Baxter, Rudy's brother.'

'Are you sure?'

'It's a long story but he came to see me in the studio a few weeks ago. He threatened me, then he sent me a letter, and there were some silent phone calls too. He followed me home and parked outside my house. He knows I had something to do with Rudy going missing.'

'Well spotted, that's his car alright. We know Martin Baxter.' says Tina. 'He's started a private prosecution against West Yorkshire police because he thinks there's some conspiracy about Rudy's disappearance. He's nothing but a pain in the backside. Leave this with me and I'll meet you back at the car.'

She pulls out her warrant card and heads towards where Martin is parked. I force myself to turn the other way and walk the few yards to our cars; seconds later the Mercedes accelerates past in a shower of gravel. Behind the wheel Martin's expression is twisted and murderous.

'What did you do?' I ask Tina when she returns.

'Don't worry,' she says. 'He won't bother us again.'

My passport arrives two weeks later and the first thing I do is to grimace at the photo: I look pale and haggard and about sixty, but there's no time to dwell on it, there's so much to do before I can go away.

I think back to Maggie's interpretation of The Hanged Man and the link to my nightmares. *Enlightenment through hanging*, she said, and maybe she has a point. I never mentioned the dreams to her and I wonder how she does it.

The bones on Baildon Moor seem to be old news now and I'm surprised there are no more reports in the papers of any other bones being found, nor any speculation on who the skeleton might be. I'm surprised Martin hasn't come forward to claim that the body as Rudy – I suppose there are formalities to go through first – but I'm sure it won't be long before his identity is officially confirmed.

I wonder if Tina knows anything so I call her mobile, but it's switched off and goes straight to voicemail; it occurs to me that it's her work phone so I don't leave a message. I try the other number on the card but the receptionist who answers tells me Tina isn't available and can't tell me when she will be back; I decline her offer of leaving a message and hang up.

I think again about her words: *Rudy deserved it...I would have done the same in your position*, but despite Tina's reassurances I still need to get away. Whether or not travelling will give me the perspective I need to achieve enlightenment is debateable, but some time away can only be a good thing.

I search online for travel options and there's so many places to choose from I can't decide where to go. I think about Spain: at least it's warm this time of year but it's too close to home: I could be back within an afternoon. The States is a possibility – and New

York is vaguely appealing – but on the other hand I want somewhere I can relax and kick back and it doesn't quite fit the bill.

New Zealand it is then: it's a good a place as any, and as far from Bradford as I can get. I book a one-way ticket to Auckland and tell Esme that I'll be back in the summer.

I clean the cottage from top to bottom and finally take the bags of clothes to the charity shops in town. There's stuff in there that hasn't seen the light of day since West Bowling: a pair of thigh-length black suede boots, a black velvet dress, and my old bike jacket. The leather is dusty with mildew and cracked with neglect and the Sydenham Poyntz logo painted on the back has peeled and faded. I go through the pockets before I put it in the charity bag and find a crumpled band flyer with a shopping list written on the back in Sullivan's perfect cursive writing. I put it in the recycling.

I go through the metal trunk under the bed, and put the old photographs and letters to one side. I separate out the photos – apart from the handful of me, Sullivan, Billy and the band they are mostly old snaps from early days at uni, of people I haven't thought of for over twenty years and will never see again. I put them all in the bin too, along with the letters. A homemade copy of a Cocteau Twins cassette, in a hand-painted purple case and labelled in gold pen – unplayed in an eternity, if ever – lays forgotten amongst them.

Somewhere near the bottom of the drift of papers I see a pale blue envelope with Sullivan's writing on, and my old address in halls of residence. I pull the sheets of lined paper from the envelope (that lovely handwriting again, in the blue ink that he always used) but I feel nothing. The paper smells musty: damp and dead.

Once everything I don't need is in storage and the cottage is spotless, I call up the lettings agency to make arrangements to rent it out. I debate about telling them that it's only a short let, but then decide against it. Something tells me that despite what I promised Esme about coming back in the summer, I won't be home for a while.

The agency sends me a nice young couple who are relocating from Liverpool. She works in sales and he's got a job at the university.

As soon as they arrive, Marwood runs upstairs and hides under my bed.

'I'm sorry. He's not very good with strangers.'

'Isn't it lovely?' she says as I show them round.

'Two up and one down,' I say. 'Compact and bijou, as the estate agents say.'

We all laugh and agree they can move in a fortnight's time.

Chapter Twenty-Seven

December 2013

It's a strange few days before I leave. I'm in limbo and camping out in my own home; almost everything is in storage apart from the clothes and other belongings that I plan to take with me to New Zealand. Already the place feels cast off, as if it's no longer mine. Marwood knows something is happening and he hardly leaves my side: he follows me around at home like a silent black shadow and I wake up every morning to find him asleep on the pillow next to me.

The Yellow Room feels odd, too. On my last day at work I spend the morning walking around the studio as if I'm seeing it for the first time. I think about the changes the place has witnessed over the years: from the advert for a junior assistant, earning next to nothing for sweeping the floors, making the tea and drawing on designs for Gary to ink; learning the trade myself and remembering how nervous I was when I picked up a tattoo machine for the first time; all the hours that I put into the final transformation from Gary's to the Yellow Room.

I look through the cuttings file that we keep in the desk drawer and find Janie Ross's article that started it all and saved the studio from folding: re-reading the interview makes me laugh and then cry in turn; we sound so optimistic and naïve. Esme and I both look so young in the photos and there's a hunted look in my eyes; a wariness that I never noticed at the time. I'm horrified by how thin I was too; my skinniness accentuated by my short hair and the black cropped top I'm wearing.

I put the folder back where it belongs with a wistful smile. The Yellow Room is a part of me and I'll miss it like crazy, but it's time for me to move on.

The next morning I put Marwood in his cat carrier and drive round to Esme's house with him on the passenger seat and his litter tray and a bag of cat food in the back. He's upset and unsettled – he associates the car with trips to the vet's – and he meows all the way as if the world is about to end. Twice he sticks his paw out of the front of the box and swipes my hand with his claws when I change gear; the second time he draws blood.

Once we get to Esme's, I let him out of the box and he jumps onto the sofa, pausing first to scratch the velvet arm.

'You wouldn't believe the noise he made all the way here,' I say to her. 'He knows something's the matter: I think he's missing me already.'

'Have you been a naughty boy, Marwood?' Esme coos and scratches his chin.

Marwood ignores me and instead he climbs onto Esme's lap, puts a huge black paw on her chest and starts to purr. I feel a stab of jealously at his flexible loyalties.

'Or maybe someone won't miss me after all.'

'I'll miss you,' says Esme.

I suddenly want to cry and panicky doubt twists my stomach. 'I'll be back before you know it. And we can Skype each other.'

'I know, but...'

'Am I really doing the right thing?'

'Of course you are, Ju. Why?'

I sit down heavily in the armchair and gaze at Marwood, asleep in Esme's lap. 'I feel as if I'm running away. I'm worried about leaving you in the lurch.'

'Oh, don't be daft. I can't remember the last time you had a holiday.'

'We went to Brighton that time.'

'That was for the tattoo convention. When was it, six, seven years ago? Come on, this is the opportunity of a lifetime. Don't worry about me and Marwood, we'll be fine.'

'Are you sure?'

'I'm sure. Now, do you want a lift to the airport tomorrow morning? Say half past six?'

I don't sleep much: the cottage is empty and echoing and without Marwood it really doesn't feel like home any more, so I'm awake and dressed an hour before Esme is due. Whilst I wait for her I stand in the back garden in the cold and look around, gazing at the stars and trying to commit the view of this corner of Bradford to memory.

When she arrives we put my suitcase in the boot and I take a final look around the cottage and lock up. In a moment of impulse I throw my door keys through the letterbox and they land with a clatter on the carpet.

I get in the car and we drive in silence through the dark. I'm nervously excited but I don't want to say so in front of Esme: as it is I feel guilty for leaving her behind and letting my excitement show would only rub it in. Instead I watch the scenery flicker past us: a country pub with an early-morning delivery of beer barrels, a train clattering northwards below us, the River Aire in full spate.

There's hardly any traffic and the journey to Leeds-Bradford airport takes us less than twenty minutes.

'Do you want a coffee? I've got over an hour yet.'

She yawns. 'That would be great, thanks.'

We find a coffee shop where I order two Americanos. I pick up a copy of the *Telegraph & Argus* whilst I wait, but I barely have time to look at the headlines on the front page before the barista calls my order. I put the paper in my bag and take our drinks over to the table.

'Thanks. You have got your passport, haven't you?'

'You asked me that half an hour ago.' I pat my shoulder bag.

'Tickets?'

I point to my bag again. 'All here.'

'You'll let me know when you've arrived?' says Esme.

'I'll email you as soon as I'm checked into the hotel. It'll probably be a couple of days what with the change at Amsterdam and the time difference.'

'Oh, Ju, I'm going to miss you so much. The studio won't be the same without you.'

'I know, I'll miss you too. But you'll be alright: text me if there's anything you need. And don't forget to give Marwood a cuddle from me.'

‘I won’t forget,’ says Esme. She flicks a tear from her cheek and I blow steam off my coffee and pretend not to notice.

‘You will be alright, won’t you? Running the Yellow Room by yourself?’

‘It’s going to be weird not having you around – but yes, I’ll be fine.’

‘Good. You’ll do a great job, I know you will.’

We linger over our drinks until the tannoy calls my flight number and it finally sinks in that I really am about to fly to the other side of the world. When we hug goodbye we’re both crying.

‘See you in the summer,’ sniffs Esme. She wraps her arms round me and squeezes me so tightly I can hardly breathe.

‘See you later.’ I walk to the departure gate and give her a final wave.

Somewhere over the Humber Estuary I unbuckle my seatbelt and relax. I’m surprised that I’m not in the slightest bit nervous of flying: in fact I’m enjoying the novelty of it. The business-suited man next to me in the aisle seat has his eyes closed and his tie is at half-mast; he’s plugged into his iPod and is oblivious to anyone or anything.

I stare out of the window. The plane is still climbing and we are surrounded by feathery clouds like wisps of smoke; I can feel the tension leave my neck and shoulders and despite the cramped seat I start to feel the stress of the past few months drain away. With every passing mile Bradford fades like a forgotten dream and it feels like it’s someone else’s life that I’m leaving behind. I think about Sullivan but for the first time I can’t remember his voice or quite recall his face; I’m surprised to find that it doesn’t bother me.

Only now I've got time to reflect do I realise the sacrifices that Tina must have made to join the police and how much she suffered because of Rudy and her childhood, and how her unwavering devotion to Billy meant she was closer to him than his own brother. I finally realise the extent of her complicity in the investigation into Rudy's disappearance and the discovery of his bones on the moor. Although she had her own reasons too, I'm amazed at how lucky I was that she was dealing with the case: I can't even start to imagine how things would have ended otherwise. I hope the police will let Rudy's family have a funeral soon; Martin may be deluded but at least he deserves that.

I wonder what New Zealand has in store for me. I've booked a hotel in Auckland for four nights but have deliberately made no other firm plans. This unfamiliar lack of purpose slightly unsettles me but at the same time it's liberating, which is a wonderful feeling. I should have done this years ago.

Perhaps I'll sign up for some History of Art classes at a local college as a way of meeting people; I'm sure I've forgotten more than I ever learned at university. Maybe I'll rent a studio in the artists' quarter of the city: not the Yellow Room Mark Two, but something different to prove that I've moved on at last. Perhaps I'll get some part-time freelance work instead: I don't want to be tied down.

Maybe I'll do something completely different: perhaps I'll open a little beach café that sells good coffee and home–made cakes and spend my spare time swimming in the sea and painting watercolours of the sparkling ocean and lush green hills. When I close my eyes I can almost feel the sun and sea breeze on my face.

I spend a few more minutes gazing at the aquamarine sky and the shifting clouds and I relax even more: the thought of having some sort of future at last is like a drug; I'm more content than I have been in longer than I can remember. I'd forgotten what happy felt like.

The clatter of the trolley and the noise of the cabin crew serving refreshments distract me from my daydreams, so I order a cup of coffee and some breakfast. I take the unread *Telegraph & Argus* from my bag and skim-read the front page (a brutal murder in Shipley; four people have been arrested after a street robbery) and turn to page two.

When I see the headline the sudden shock is like a steel trap slamming around my heart. I want to scream but suddenly I can't breathe.

Bradford Telegraph & Argus

19 December 2013

Baildon Moor Skeleton Identified as Missing Pudsey Man

West Yorkshire Police have confirmed the identity of the man whose remains were found by a dog-walker at an isolated beauty spot near Bradford last autumn.

Joe Simmonds (28), who had been reported missing by his family after a night out on New Year's Eve 1999, was conclusively identified using DNA and dental records.

'At last we can put this behind us and move on,' his father Jim told the *Telegraph & Argus.* 'It's been terrible all this time, not knowing what happened to our Joe but now we can say goodbye properly.'

An inquest returned a verdict of accidental death. The coroner stated that it was likely that Mr Simmonds had become lost whilst taking a short cut home across the moors after celebrating with friends and suffered fatal injuries as a result of a fall.

The funeral will take place at Nab Wood Crematorium on Monday 30th December. Family flowers only please.

Made in the USA
Columbia, SC
28 July 2017